I0630718

Instant Billionaire

DEEP DARK SECRETS
BOOK ONE

J.J. LOVE

SIMONE FOX

CRAVE PUBLISHING

Instant Billionaire

Copyright © 2023 by J.J. Love and Simone Fox

All rights reserved.

First Print Edition: January 2023

Crave Publishing

Kailua, HI 96734

www.cravepublishing.net

Formatting: Crave Publishing

ISBN-13: 978-1-64034-658-1

No part of this book may be reproduced, scanned, or distributed in any printed or electronic form without permission. Please do not participate in or encourage piracy of copyrighted materials in violation of the author's rights. Thank you for respecting the hard work of this author.

This is a work of fiction. Names, characters, places, and incidents either are the product of the author's imagination or are used fictitiously, and any resemblance to locales, events, business establishments, or actual persons—living or dead—is entirely coincidental.

CHAPTER 1

Johnathan

"ONE CARAMEL LATTE with a shot of expresso!"

The coffee shop bustles with the usual energy of a Monday morning. Baristas behind the counter dash back and forth as customers wait in an impatient clump buried deep in their phones. I lean against the far wall and check my own screen for comfort.

A few years ago, there was no shortage of excitement blowing up my phone. Girls, parties, and endless nights of fun. I can close my eyes and still see Jenny Malt stripping on the dining room table at three in the morning. Now I'm just the guy seven years into a loveless marriage waiting for his coffee.

Oh, how hard the mighty fall.

"Johnathan," the barista calls.

I raise my hand and walk toward the counter, wading through the crowd. Guess it's back to the office for another mediocre work week. I wonder what my old man has planned for me today. Probably another meeting. Another sales pitch. I wonder how pissed he'd be if I invited a stripper to liven things up?

A blue-suited guy snatches my cup up before I can finish crossing through the crowd.

"Hey, buddy. Try stealing someone else's coffee," I yell.

I grip the man's shoulder to stop him, but my cup is already pressed to his lips. He eyes me with a mischievous smile, his face quickly distorting into disgust as he sticks out his tongue. "Ew, what is this? Black?"

I refrain from smacking him upside the head and snatch back my coffee with a smirk. "What the fuck are you doing here?"

"Questioning an old friend on their taste in coffee," Jax muses, throwing a casual arm over my shoulder.

Jax Baxter. The last person I expected to see today but I'm glad I did.

He stares at me. "I haven't seen you in a while. You look exhausted."

"No more than I did in law school." I shrug.

"Still working for that brute you call a father?"

I nod. "Got three more years before I get to move up."

"Well, a few minutes with an old friend isn't gonna break your schedule, is it?"

I'm tempted to check the time. I can already hear

my dad yelling at me the moment I walk through the door of his office. Whether I'm on time or not doesn't really matter. He just likes to yell. I shrug. "It wouldn't kill me."

We weave back through the masses to a table by the window. The New York foot traffic zooms by outside, and I settle into the cushion-backed chair with ease. Normally I'd be one of those hurried blobs of gray, eager to get to my destination. Every. Single. Day.

"So where's your wife been hiding you, man?" he asks. "I haven't seen you since the wedding."

Ah, yes. The famous business transaction everyone likes to call my marriage. Three more years and the contract will finally expire. I'll be a free man. Not that I'd burden Jax with any of this.

"You know how my dad is. Work till you can't and then work some more."

Jax stares at me. "You look like you've been hit by a truck."

"Burn out doesn't age well," I chuckle, taking in his fresh expression. "You look well."

He leans back in his chair, pompous as ever. "Oh, go on."

"Seriously, man. Whatever you're doing I need it in bulk."

"Same thing I've always done." He shrugs and pulls a muffin out of his bag.

"You still do those weekend trips?"

He points the top of his muffin at me. "Do you

have any idea how demanding the attorney general's office is? Without those weekend getaways, I'd look worse than you." He unwraps it and pops a piece in his mouth, the faint smell of blueberry lingering as he leans the rest my way. Just like old times.

I break off a piece of the muffin top as the old memories resurface. Back to those burned-out college days. Back to weekend trips blowing off steam at some nearby island.

"Some of my best mistakes were on those weekend trips," I muse. "Sadly, those days seem like a million years ago."

"That's it." He slams his hand on the table. "That's exactly what you need. Sandy beaches. Sexy girls."

I take a sip of my coffee. "Keep dreaming, Jax. My dad has my schedule locked tighter than jail."

"Well, make time, man, because I happen to have an extra ticket to paradise with your name on it."

I blink at him as he breaks off another piece of muffin. "Oh, really? And where are we going?"

"To an all-expenses-paid resort in Puerto Rico." He cheers, flinging crumbs across the table. "My cousin is getting married this weekend, and I already signed up for a plus-one."

I smirk. "No hot date for Jax Baxter?"

He drapes the back of his hand on his forehead. "Sadly, this city isn't a fan of my romantic reputation. I'll just have to find some exotic beauty to woo once we get there."

"I'm in. I could use a break from my dad's hellish work ethic."

"Then it's settled." He whips out his phone. "I'll send you the information now."

Excitement flows through me as we update our contacts. Leave it to Jax to swoop in and save the day after all these years.

"I'm so glad I ran into you. It's gonna be just like old times! Jax and Johnathan back by popular demand." He raises his muffin high in the air, laughing as a few other customers give us strange looks.

"They won't know what hit 'em." I raise my coffee cup in salute.

No sooner do I down the last of the delicious bitterness does my phone vibrate across the table, my father's scowling face lighting up the screen.

"Well, that was short lived." I sigh, forwarding it to voicemail.

"You'll be on those sandy shores soon enough man." Jax's face creases with empathy, the years that have passed slightly visible. I guess we both needed a vacation.

"Not soon enough." I stand, looking at him. "If you don't send me the itinerary for this trip, I promise I will hunt you down."

"Don't worry." He laughs. "I've got you."

"You better." I throw my cup in the trash and give him a wave before walking out onto the busy side-walk. The last time I went on a vacation was for my bogus honeymoon where my new bride sat in the shade the whole time and slept in a separate bed. No sex. Not even a kiss or two to wet my dreams. But that was all about to change on this trip.

I don't even care what my pseudo wife has to say. Or my dad. Distance will be greatly welcomed from this monotonous life. It will be good to get out of this city and sit on the beach with my toes in the sand instead under a mound of papers. And if I manage to snag a woman with my charm, it will be a welcomed distraction. My pants become tighter at the thought, and I continue my way toward my father's empire with nearly a skip in my step. For just a moment, the party king will return. And, this time, he will not be silenced.

CHAPTER 2

Kylie

FINALLY!

The humid air of the island clings to my jetlagged body as I yank my suitcase out of the trunk of the cab. As beautiful as this island is, I can do with a little less sweating and a little more help. The cool air of the lobby beckons me as the automatic doors open for a couple walking hand in hand. The love in their eyes makes me sick. I should tell them that it won't last. It never does. He'll probably sneak a few glances at the other girls when she's not looking. But other people's love lives are not the goal of my weekend. This trip is all about me. Nothing like those business trips that my husband called a vacation. This time, I'm a free woman. No more polite conversation with the head boss at dinner while my husband flirts with the waitress. I refuse to let anyone shackle me down for anything ever again.

The opportunity for fun and adventure is out there waiting for me, and I'm going to find it.

I slam the trunk closed, and an island breeze whips through my hair, cooling the back of my neck. I doubt rich Debra will even notice I'm here amid the chaos of her special day. It's not like we're ever that close. But when someone invites you on a free trip to Puerto Rico, you take it. Even if it is for something as repulsive as a wedding.

I hike my bag up higher on my shoulder as I clunk up the last step. The sliding glass doors part with a burst of AC, the chandelier glittering above as I stroll to the front desk. Judging by the clock on the wall, there's just enough time for me to settle in before the big "I Do's." No way am I going to waste it a moment of it. There's nothing better than having food and drink on someone else's dime. The only thing that would make this weekend better would be snagging a hot guy for a night or two.

"Next guest in line." A woman waves at me from behind the counter.

No sooner do I walk forward does someone else's shoulder slam into mine. My bag clatters to the ground, causing a few heads to turn and stare. I glare at the guy buried in his phone as he mumbles a quick sorry before walking off, the scent of coffee and cologne wafting by.

Typical. I rush to gather my things and walk over to the counter.

"GIVE it up for the bride and groom!"

The crowd cheers as the lucky couple walks in, Debra's white dress a mass of ruffles and fabrics. Better her than me. I take another sip of my wine and do my best to smile and play along. I hate weddings. Everything about them screams fake happiness. Even the married couples sitting at the tables wear fake smiles. But you can see it in their eyes. They're desperate to hide the truth of what awaits the newlyweds after today. The sadness. The frustration. The silent cry for help because they no longer know who they are as individuals. From here on out, they're just Mr. and Mrs.

That was me once. So naïve and in love. Glad that's over with.

The cool night air blows through the palm trees as everyone continues to cheer, and I check my phone for the fifteenth time. My brother was supposed to be here by now. Is this how things are going to be when I move in next week? The mere thought of moving makes me want to squeal, my smile barely containing my excitement. Finally, after an eternity of textbooks and late-night binges, I finally have my Masters. Not that I got a fancy party like this to celebrate. I guess those are only reserved for when you throw your life way.

It didn't take my brother much convincing for me to agree living out in a big city. When you're in the real estate business, a city is practically a beacon. And I'm ready to take it head on. If only he'd pick up his phone. The movers had taken the last of my things from my apartment before I left, so I want to make sure they got there okay. Maybe one more text will get his attention.

"Woohoo."

I snap my head up from my screen, the sound of a half-hearted cheer piquing my interest. Is there someone else around that isn't slathered in the adrenaline of marriage? I down my glass and take another from a passing tray as I scan the crowd. He stands a few high tops away, eyes glued to his phone as he half-heartedly waves his hand in the air. The same way he looked earlier when he slammed into me in the lobby. I'm irritated and intrigued at the same time.

Of course, the only other cynic of love at this stupid reception is Mr. Phone Zombie. I watch him over the rim of my glass as he glances up and looks around. He's tall, hands tugging at his tie with a scowl on his angular face. He's looking for an escape. Just like me.

Maybe I should go up to him. I mean, we're on one of the most beautiful beaches in the world. And there's no use in letting a hot guy go to waste, right? I take another sip of liquid courage before walking over. This weekend is going to be different. No matter what.

CHAPTER 3

Johnathan

I TUG AT MY TIE, uncomfortable as ever. I can't take this much longer. Every second standing here only reminds me of my own caged nightmare. All the white ruffles and flowers send shivers down my spine. I want to scream at the groom dancing with his new wife to run and never look back. But by the look of the woman in white, she doesn't seem like too much of a tight ass. Unlike my own vulture in disguise who doesn't even bother picking up when I call her. I sigh, amused at my own thoughts. So much for getting away from it all.

I check my phone again, hopeful that a message from Jax has arrived. But it hasn't. He called me last night to complain about his cancelled flight, but I thought he'd at least make it to the reception. Unless he hooked up with a Caribbean babe the second he walked off the plane. Not that I'd be surprised.

I look again. Still, no message. I'm going to kill

him. I look around at the guests and tug at my tie a second time. I know Jax said to stay for the free cocktails, but this is too much to bear alone. I doubt anyone will notice if I leave before dinner.

"Are you always this enthused?"

I'm brought back to reality by a dark-haired beauty dressed in red. Even in the dim candlelight I can tell her cheeks are flushed. Her dress hugs her curved body in all the right places, that plunging neckline beckoning me to stay. I guess a few more minutes won't hurt.

"Weddings aren't really my thing," I say, sliding my phone in my back pocket.

"Believe me. This is the last place I want to be right now."

"Are you here for the bride or the groom?" I muse.

She leans forward, tits pushed up again the high top. "I'm here for the free food like everyone else."

"And booze. Don't forget booze."

Her golden eyes glaze me over with a nod. "I'm glad we have a chance to properly meet."

"I'm sorry, have we met before?" I extend my hand her way. "I think I would've remembered someone as beautiful as you."

"I'm the one you nearly knocked down in the lobby." She shakes my hand with the force of a man. The vague memory of bumping into someone resurfaces. After living in the city, small bumps in public are so common they're almost inevitable. I guess this woman doesn't feel the same way.

"Ah." I clear my throat. "Well, I do remember that. Sorry."

"I think I'll be able to forgive you if you continue to keep me company."

Her hand falls back around the stem of her glass, and I watch her lips wrap around the rim.

"I welcome the company." I smile. "Not many people here seem too excited to talk to the family friend."

"That's because they're all still sober. Give them an hour and they'll be all over you."

For the first time in a while, I feel more like myself. Easy conversation with a beautiful woman is nice. No work, or work talk. And the thought of having that sexy, little body all over me makes my insides stir. It's been a while since I've felt like this. I must be way more stressed than I thought. I down my abandoned champagne from the earlier toast and clear my throat. "Is this your first time in Puerto Rico?"

She shakes her head. "No, but the past few times were on less enjoyable terms. I'm hoping to make this trip a good one."

I steal a glass off a passing tray and hold it in the air. "I'll drink to that."

We clink our glasses and drink in comfortable silence. The bride and groom feed each other cake in the distance, the bride laughing as cake is smeared on her nose. If I'd done that to Isabella, she would've stabbed me with the cake knife. Missed opportunities.

"The stars sure are beautiful tonight."

I glance up at the collection of lights dancing above us. Right. Stars. "Sometimes I forget that the stars even exist," I admit. "Back home it's nothing but tall buildings and airplanes."

"Oh, a city man?" she asks but doesn't seem too pressed for the details. Her gaze tells it all. I almost feel like prey, and I welcome the change of pace.

"Guilty as charged." I smile, eyes resting back on her.

Wow, she's beautiful. Maybe it's the combination of the ocean waves and the champagne, but I can't help but find her tantalizing. Nothing like Isabella. This girl is a firecracker. The energy of her hand inches from mine is infectious. She's a woman who knows exactly what she wants. I think I want her too. Normally I wouldn't even entertain the idea of another woman for fear of adding more complexity to my already complicated life. But something about this seems effortless. Like a home away from home. Maybe Jax was right. This trip is long overdue. I can't help but lean in closer, brushing a few stray hairs out of her eyes.

"Is it hard to find good company in the city?" she breathes.

"Yes."

It's an honest answer. Ever since I got married, it

seems like everyone in my life suddenly evaporated. First Jax, then the rest of the frat followed. And forget about even trying to touch the viper queen. There's a reason she arranged to stay in an apartment not too far from mine. If I had to see that scowling face every day and wasn't getting laid, I'd be in the afterlife with ol' Grandpa Joe. But this woman in front of me makes all those worries melt away.

"Want to skip dinner?" she asks, finger lightly tracing the back of my hand. "I think I have something back in my hotel that might be a bit tastier."

It takes everything I have to restrain myself as I lace my fingers with hers. The rest of the party melts away as I press my lips to her ear, pants tighter than ever.

"Lead the way."

CHAPTER 4

Kylie

WAS I really doing this right now?

I keep my head low as I lead my mystery man through the throng of people. Thank goodness everyone is too busy looking at the happy couple to notice us. The last thing I need is Aunt Gertie ruining the mood with her invasive questions. My heartbeat is all that I can hear by the time we make it to the elevator. It's been a while since I've been alone with a guy. Not since my minute-man of a husband. And with my studies not leaving much time left for socializing, I can't even remember the last time I was alone with a guy. But this isn't just any guy.

I sneak a quick glance and suck in a breath. God, he's gorgeous. The perfect mixture of mysterious and sexy that must lure in hundreds of girls. Even intoxicated, he's going to notice how inexperienced I am. I still have time to back out and make up some lame excuse. But as the doors to the elevator ding open, I know that there's no reason for me to run. He tightens his grip on my hand and leads me inside, eyes luring me forward. Inexperienced or not, I want him.

"Which floor is yours?" he asks, fingers hovering over the buttons.

I don't hesitate to brush my fingers against his and click the twelfth floor. His touch is electric. Yep, I'm really doing this. His hand presses into the small of my back and draws me closer, giving me goose-bumps. Is he about to start right here in the elevator? God, I hope so.

Suddenly the elevator bell dings and the doors open. "'Scuse us."

His touch retreats as I press my back into the wall to make room for the elderly couple walking on. Great, an audience. I sigh as the doors slide closed behind them, and we ride up together in silence. I can feel his hand grazing mine with antici-pation. I do my best not to squirm next to him as the couple goes on and on about gift shop toothpaste. Only a few more flights and I'll have him all to myself.

It takes all of my strength to refrain from bull-dozing the elderly couple as soon as the doors open. He doesn't let go of me as I lead him down the hall. My panties are soaked by the time we reach the door, and I fumble to find the key card in my purse. His hands grab at my hips, bringing him closer. Deeper. Focus, Kylie. His cock twitches on my ass, demanding that I get us inside as I yank out the key card in victory. I hold it up against the sensor as his breath lingers on my ear.

"I can't hold back for much longer," he growls.

The door can't open fast enough, and I jump a little as it slams closed behind us, shrouding the room in complete darkness.

His lips are on the back of my neck as I turn the lock, fingers working the zipper of my dress down my spine. The darkness heightens every sense of his touch as my dress falls away.

His breath on my shoulders ignites goosebumps across my skin.

His lips press against my ear. "My turn."

I'm breathless as I spin to face him. Even in the darkness I can make out the lust clouding his eyes. I run my hands down his chest and press my lips against his as I charm each button undone. His tongue finds mine, my back melting into the wall as he devours me. His shirt falls away, and I wrestle with the belt buckle and his tongue all at once. This is different from anyone I've ever been with. Stranger or not, I want all of him inside me. I slide the zipper down his pants and brush my fingers against his bulging cock. A shiver runs through him. There's nothing holding me back, but I can't help but relish in the tease, the fabric of his pants soft on my palm as I stroke him a few times. So big. I want to enjoy every second of this.

My back slides down the wall, my mouth

watering as I drop his pants to the floor to reveal all of him. My tongue trails down the tip slowly, and his hand grips the wall above me for support. I slide down further. The taste of him drives me wild, and I can't help but moan as his fingers run through my hair and tugs slightly.

"Don't stop," he growls, pushing himself deeper.

His cock completely fills my throat as I move faster. No way am I planning on stopping anytime soon. The faint smell of coffee, booze, and cologne swirls around me. His taste is addicting as I release him and slide my tongue down to his balls. I won't stop until I've had my fill of him.

He escapes from my slippery grasp, breath ragged as he stares me down. I lick my lips and rest on my heels, grateful for the wall's support. "I thought you didn't want me to stop?"

"Bed," he growls, cock twitching in the darkness. "Now."

I silently comply and stumble toward the queen-size pillowtop not too far away. Even it's been a while since I've gone this far with a man, he doesn't seem to notice. Just the thought of him inside me is enough to make me burst.

"How do you want me?" My voice trembles as I sit on the edge of the bed.

He towers above me, everything about him ravenous for more. "Just as you are."

His lips are back on mine, and he guides me back into the sheets, our tongues intertwined once more.

I press myself against him, ready for more. His hands are beside my head as he pulls away and looks down at me with a smirk. His chest hovers over mine as the rest of him presses against my soaked panties.

"I want you every way," he whispers, fingers sliding the damp fabric onto the floor.

My eyes cross as his fingers slide inside of me. "Oh, god."

"Don't hold yourself back," he growls, moving faster. "I want you to cum to your heart's desire."

His words alone leave me helpless, lips trailing down my body until his tongue lands on my clit. Every circle drives me wild. My back arches as my juices soak the sheets, but he doesn't stop. I'm trembling by the time he sits back and eyes me, licking his fingers with a devilish smile. He's toying with me. A hunter playing with his food. I stare at him in anticipation for more. Now I'm the prey. And I love every moment of it.

CHAPTER 5

Johnathan

HER JUICES DRIP into my mouth like the sweetest honey.

God, she tastes divine. Nothing short of heaven stares back at me as she lays there trembling, her curved body entangled with the sheets. I tug at the cup of her bra and run my tongue across her nipple, her moans like music to my ears. She fumbles with the clasp and rips it off of her.

It's been so long since I've tasted pussy that I can't even hide how much I'm enjoying this. I dive back in and lap at her insides.

She clings to the sheets. "More!" she screams. "More."

God, what I wouldn't give for her to scream my name. But now is not the time for introductions. I twist her nipples hard as my tongue swirls around her clit. I can't hold back anymore. I need be inside her.

I lick my lips and look down at her as I slide inside.

Fuck, she feels so good. My hands frame her face, the picture of ecstasy written across it as I go deeper inside her.

"Yes!" she screams, legs wrapping around me. "Fuck, yes."

The faint scent of lavender still lingers on her skin as I suck on her neck. It's going to be impossible to say goodbye to this in the morning. But for now, I'm going to enjoy every inch of her until she tells me to stop.

THE SUN nearly blinds me as I wake up to the sound of my phone buzzing near my ear. No doubt it's Jax wonder where the hell I ended up last night. I blindly reach for the phone and answer.

"Yo," I mumble, head pounding as I walk to the bathroom. No use waking up my mystery girl over this.

"Is that any way to greet your mother?"

Great. Just the person I wanted to hear from on vacation. "Sorry, Mom. I thought you were—"

"Your father is in the hospital. He had a heart attack last night."

I close the door of the bathroom. "Oh?"

"Johnathan! Your father just suffered a heart attack and all you can say is oh?" she yells. "No one's been able to get ahold of you for hours. I need you here now."

"Mom, I'm not in New York, but I'll be there as soon as I can."

"What do you mean? What else could you possibly have to do that's more important?"

"I have a life, you know."

"If your father dies without you being here, I'll never forgive you."

The line goes dead. I drop the phone on the counter and splash some water on my face. The countertop is cool on my palms as I grip the edge of the sink and stare at my bloodshot eyes, nothing but fear looking back at me. There's no way that the old man can croak now. Not before I cancel this whole business deal with the viper queen. I glance down at the blinking screen to see several missed calls and texts from various people. The whole idea of dealing with any of this makes me want to crawl back into bed with my mystery woman and restart tomorrow. But life has other plans for me as my phone vibrates with another incoming message.

I make my way back out to the room and immediately admire every inch of her. That dark hair falls around her body as she snuggles deeper into the sheets. What I wouldn't give to make her mine for more than a night. I shrug back into my clothes with a heavy sigh. Maybe I should leave a note or something. If my old man wasn't trying to die on us, I would totally slide back in for seconds. But I think better of it and choose to slink out the door. Better to leave as a mystery guy than as anyone else. Especially for her sake. The last thing I need is to ruin someone else's life with my family's drama. No matter how much I loved last night, she doesn't deserve to be tangled up in my fucking mess. I pick up my shirt, and a clutch purse comes tumbling out, a cell phone thumping loudly to the floor. Crap. I look back, expecting her eyes to shoot open, but she still lays asleep as if nothing happened. Good. The last thing I need is to explain any of this right now.

I slide her phone on the nightstand and throw the clutch on the chair. Goodbye, mystery girl. I can't help but steal one last look before shrugging on my shirt and walking out the door. So much for a vacation.

THE HOSPITAL HALLWAY is silent as I'm led to my father's room by one of his men. Apparently, they requested the whole floor to be cleared out for privacy. Leave it to my dad to flaunt his wealth even at the end. The door opens, and I'm frozen at the sight. Wires and tubes stick out of my dad from every angle. The pompous asshat that I expected to see is now just this frail-looking raisin being held up by tubes. Is this really my dad?

"Johnathan." My mom leaps up from her seat. "You sure took your sweet time getting here."

"I was on a plane, Mom. It's not like I was in Jersey."

"Of all the times to be out partying." She scoffs.

"Oh, like I knew the old man was going to have a heart attack the moment I left."

"Can we have the room for a moment?" My dad's voice is low but strong.

My mom instantly shuts up and nods. "Of course."

She follows a few other men back out of the room, glaring at me as she closes the door. As if I'm so privileged to be alone with him.

"Come here."

He doesn't move much because of the wires, but as I inch closer, I brace for a slap out of habit.

I kneel by his bed. "What's up, Dad?"

"I'm sorry, Johnathan," he whispers. "I tried it get out of it, but I failed."

My heart goes into a sprint. "What do you mean?"

"Leo and his daughter. They're more dangerous than I thought." He wheezes, the monitors beside him rising sharply. "Whatever you can do to get yourself out, do it."

"Dad?" My hands shake as he coughs violently. "Dad, what are you saying?"

"The business is in your hands now, son." He grabs my hand in his. "Do whatever it takes to keep safe."

His coughing continues, and I press the emergency button by his bed. The monitors continue to beep around me as his coughing slows.

"What are you talking about? Is this about money? Dad?"

I press the button again. There's no way he's leaving me with this. What about our deal? What about my freedom?

"We had a deal!" I scream as the monitor flatlines, tears streaming down my face. The door bursts open, and a flood of nurses enters the room, but I know it's too late. One of my dad's men leads me out of the room and back into the hallway. I guess they're my men now. The tears continue to fall as I numbly sit in a plastic chair. The cold wave of reality hits me as my mom sobs uncontrollably, falling at the threshold. My dad's gone. And so is my freedom.

CHAPTER 6

Kylie

I'VE NEVER BEEN SO excited to wake up to an empty bed. The sun warms my cheeks as I squeal with glee. I can't believe I did that. And I get to avoid the awkward morning conversation? This is the best vacation ever. My phone buzzes on the nightstand. I'm pretty sure I abandoned my purse somewhere by the door. Was my mystery man nice enough to bring it over here for me? I open one eye and check the name, my brother's goofy face looking back at me. Lovely, a video call.

"Geez, you look like shit," he says as I snuggle into the covers and hide myself.

"Oh, good. You're alive." I roll my eyes. "I thought the plane you were on vanished after you ghosted me."

"Ha-ha. My flight got cancelled, and then I overslept." He shakes his head. "Just meet me in the lounge and I'll tell you over breakfast."

"I'm on my way."

I hang up the phone and roll over to the other side of the bed. The faint scent of him still lingers. I wonder why he had to go so suddenly. Normally the girl is the one trying to sneak out. Not that I'm complaining.

The memories of last night run through my mind. I thought he was going to break me in two the way he handled me. Never has a man ever made me feel so alive. Normally I'm just a shy woman on her back with not much to offer. But last night he brought something out in me that made me feel powerful. Dangerous.

I savor his scent one last time before climbing out of bed and stretch in the morning glow. A quick shower should make me hungry enough for breakfast. Time to get ready for the first day of a whole new life.

***

"AND THE PERSON next to me didn't even apologize."

The din of the café surrounds us as my brother rants on about his terrible travels.

I pour syrup on my pancakes. "Even after he drooled on you?"

"Exactly!" He flings his fork around as he talks. "How do you accidentally drool on someone anyway? This is exactly why I fly first class."

"Well, sorry for your airplane trauma, but you

missed a total flop of a wedding." I shovel a forkful of pancake in my mouth with glee.

"You think all weddings are disasters, little sister. Besides, I wasn't even mad I missed the wedding. I'm mad I missed Johnathan."

"Johnathan? Is there something you need to tell me?" I eye him.

"Hilarious." He shakes his head. "But seriously we were supposed to be kings again. Jax and Johnathan for one night only. But no. All I get is a cancelled flight and a stranger's drool on my shoulder."

"Oh, boohoo about your shoulder. Did the movers come yet?"

He smirks a little and reaches for his coffee. "Yes, Kylie. They dropped off all your stuff this morning. I promise you it's safe."

"Good." I smile. "I don't want anything going wrong once I get there."

"It's New York. Something's always going wrong."

"Well, once I start selling apartments and condos, things are going to start going right."

He shakes his head. "I'm happy that you're excited. I just want you to take it slow once you get out there. There's a lot of danger in the city, and I don't want you getting mixed up in any of it."

"Jax, you worry too much." I stuff my face with more food from the buffet with glee. Nothing tastes better than free food.

"As your big brother, I worry the right amount." He stabs his bacon with authority.

"Still using that big brother card on me?"

"Until I die." He smiles. "Seriously, though. I'm happy you're going to move in with me. I can't wait to show you around as soon as we get there."

"Yes. I want to see it all. After being trapped in school for so long, I feel like I'm finally starting my life."

A funky ringtone chimes from Jax's pocket, and he takes out his phone.

"Hey, man. I'm so sorry I bailed on ya—"

The cheerful expression suddenly falls from Jax's face as he listens. I eat my food in silence and stare at my plate. Whatever he had going on, it clearly wasn't the time for jokes.

"All right. Send me the address and I'll be there." He hangs up the phone, leaning back in his seat with a sigh.

"You okay, bro?"

"Johnathan's dad just passed, and I think he's freaking out." He rubs the bridge of his nose. "I told him I'll go to the funeral in a few days."

"Oh, okay," I say, trying to sound neutral. I'm not about to be the insensitive little sister who thinks sightseeing is more important than the funeral. Even if I am disappointed.

He looks at his phone and perks up a little. "Hey, here's a thought. Why don't you just come with me?

It probably won't be that long, and it's right by some cool spots I can show you. What do you think?"

I sip on my orange juice. "Don't you think it'll be weird to show up to a stranger's funeral?"

"People drop in to pay their respects all the time at graveyards. Plus, Johnathan and I go way back. We're practically family."

"He says to his sister." I laugh.

"Come on," he pleads, clasping his hands together. "We'll only be there for a minute. I promise."

"Well, how can I say no to that offer?" I shake my head. "Fine. Fine. I'll go."

"Yes." He leans back in his chair and shovels another forkful of food in his mouth.

I munch on a strawberry and look out the window toward the ocean. I wonder if my mystery man is still here. Maybe I can steal another moment away before I'm permanently under the watchful eye of my brother.

"So, are you just going to lounge by the pool today or what?" I ask, looking back at him.

"Absolutely not. We are going to check out some places on the island," Jax says, slamming his fist on the table with authority. "No way did I go through all this travel just to fly back empty handed. Kylie, today you will be my wingman. Tell me, which pose do you think I should go with?"

I bust out laughing as he flexes his muscles in

hilarious poses. If living with my brother was going to be this entertaining, I'm going to have a blast in New York. Even if it does have to start at a stranger's funeral.

CHAPTER 7

Johnathan

OF COURSE it would rain on the day of my old man's funeral. He never did make things easy.

The rain patters on and drips off the side of my umbrella as I stand next to the hole my dad is about to be dropped into. If he was here, he'd have someone holding an umbrella for him as he complained about the weather. Probably would've had something to say about the service too. But without him the only other sound I can hear is a group of black birds cawing from a nearby tree. It really is quiet without him.

I lift up my sleeve and check my watch. My mother should've arrived already with the rest of the procession fifteen minutes ago. She was a wreck at the funeral home and managed to make enough of a scene to be escorted away by two of Dad's men. My men. I don't think I'll be able to get used to this.

There is no way this old man left me everything. It's like the nightmare that won't end.

I glance over at my semi-somber bride standing beside me. Her face always seems in mourning, those thin lips hardly smiling or cracking any real expression. Not even at our wedding could she muster to flash a smile unless it was for the cameras. Got to keep up appearances. And today is no exception.

My father-in-law claps me on the shoulder, his meaty fingers gripping me tight. "I hope that you can see me as a reliable father figure for you, Johnathan. Anything you need, I'll be there."

"Thank you, sir," I say, numb. I can't help but think of my dad's last words. What was so bad that would make him so afraid of Leonardo Guerra?

"My shoes are getting muddy," Isabella mumbles. "How long does it take to throw someone in the ground?"

"Isabella," her father scolds her. "Your father-in-law is being buried today. Have an ounce of compassion."

"I don't see any compassion being shown for my shoes. Or to me. I'm the one standing in the rain here. He's already in the box."

"Then maybe you should just wait in the car," I spit.

She glares at me. "Gladly."

Isabella turns in a huff and wobbles away, her

heels getting trapped in the ever-growing mud. Serves her right. I don't need her setting my mother off once we get her settled. I glance at my watch again impatiently. How long does it take to sedate one woman? Any longer with this man and I might not last.

"You have to forgive Isa." Leonardo sighs. "She doesn't have a tolerance for death after her mother passed."

I nod, staring at the gaping hole below us. "Death can be a touchy subject."

"I think that it's great that your father left you everything," he continues. "Gives the transferring of it all a lighter load."

"Yeah," I say, ready to jump in the hole myself.

"Are you sure you'll be able to handle it all? If it ever becomes too much, I have a crew ready to help at any time."

I look up at him with a tight-lipped smile. "I appreciate that. It's nice to have someone you can trust so close to the family business."

He smiles. "Whatever I can do to alleviate your burden amidst this sudden tragedy."

"Johnathan!"

We both glance toward the parking lot, the sound of my mother's laughter echoing around the graveyard. Leonardo's face contorts with disgust. "I believe that your mother is in need of assistance."

Clearly. But I'm not about to go and offer my arm to her. Even if she is my mother, that woman hasn't acted like one in years. And today is not the day to start pretending.

"Would you mind helping her?" I ask. "I think she might just hit me if I try to help."

"Of course." He nods, walking away with disdain. Better him than me.

I wait until Leo's far enough away and look around for any hidden bodyguards. For once, everyone is more focused on my inebriated mother. I sigh with relief and close my eyes.

This is the first moment since my dad died that I've had to myself. I guess being the CEO of a large firm does come with a giant target on your back. But do they really have to guard me every second of the day?

I hear the sloshing of approaching footsteps and internally groan. Now what?

"Hey, man."

I open my eyes as Jax walks up beside me. The rain drips onto my jacket as he knocks my umbrella over, giving me a hug.

"Normally I have to wait until you're drunk to get one of these." I laugh, hugging him back.

"Well, today's a special occasion." He grabs both my shoulders and looks me dead in the eye. "Are you doing okay? And be honest."

The kindness in his eyes is more than I can take, and I fidget a little. "Honestly? I don't know."

As soon as they confirmed his death, I was whisked away to sign every paper they could find to transfer things to my name. Rights. Assets. Partners. It just became words on a page at some point. Another signature here, another initial there. Every movement of the pen taking more and more of my freedom away.

"Word on the street is that you're the new CEO." Jax nudges me.

I chuckle bitterly. "Word travels fast."

"I'd congratulate ya if it wasn't so—"

"Found it!"

I perk up at her voice. I must really be losing it if I'm fantasizing in the middle of the day. But the sound of sloshing grows closer. This is too real to be a fantasy.

"Took you long enough." Jax turns, waving. "Come and say hi so we can go."

"What am I, a toddler?"

I turn, knocking my umbrella into Jax's as I watch a dark-haired beauty walking our way. She's dressed in jeans and a sweatshirt like it's just another day. Like my tongue didn't trace every inch of her body a few nights ago. This is no hallucination. There is no way it's possible and yet here she is walking toward me. My mystery girl.

CHAPTER 8

Kylie

THIS HAS to be some kind of cosmic joke. I can almost hear the laughter as my eyes lock with his across the scattered tombstones. There is no way that the guy my brother wouldn't shut up about all morning is the same guy as my mystery man. Part of me wants to turn around and walk back to the car, but my brother ushers me along.

"Hurry up, slowpoke!"

I do my best to hurry through the mud and manage to finally reach them.

"Sorry, mud's a little slippery over there." I sigh, looking between them. "What did I miss?"

My mystery man shifts uncomfortably as I stand next to Jax. I can see that he hasn't forgotten our night together. So much for avoiding an awkward conversation.

"Kylie, this is the guy I spent the best years of my

life with, Johnathan Ronsberry. Johnathan, this is my pain-in-the-ass little sister, Kylie."

"Really, my whole name?" He shakes his head with a smirk and sticks out his hand to me. "I'm glad we have a chance to properly meet."

I suppress a smile as I firmly shake his hand. "I'm sorry, have we met before?"

"Well, Jax would often talk about a brat of a sister who lived back home."

He's playing it cool, but I can see the questions in his eyes. And he can see mine.

"And now this brat is a master's graduate and ready to take on the real estate world." Jax wraps an arm around my shoulders, knocking our umbrellas together. "Since you're new in town, we should go out to dinner. Care to grace us with your presence?"

"Oh, ugh," Johnathan stutters. "I don't know. There's still so much to deal with around here."

"And there will still be things to deal with once you've had dinner with us. Come on, it's the least I can do for leaving you this weekend."

"Don't pressure the guy." I slide out of my brother's grip and readjust my umbrella. Being this close to him is already overwhelming me enough. The last thing I need is to be trapped under my brother's sweaty armpit.

I glance over at him. Johnathan. I can't think of a better name for a man like him. If I had known, I would've screamed it all night long. The memories of that night resurface, and my cheeks flame. *Please say no. Please say no.*

"Yeah. Sure, Jax, why not?" Johnathan clears this throat and smiles at Jax. "I guess I could use a reason to escape from all of this for a minute."

"That's the spirit," Jax cheers, clapping him on the shoulder.

"Cool," I say a bit too loudly.

"Johnathan!"

I look past Johnathan to see a loud woman walking our way and waving, her other arm clinging tightly to a disgruntled-looking man.

Johnathan turns his back to us and shakes his head with a groan. "Is she seriously drunk right now?"

"You need me to stay for support?" Jax asks.

"Nah, you guys get out of here and enjoy the day. I'll deal with my mother." Johnathan's eyes fall on me as he faces us before looking at Jax. He sticks his hand out between them with tired smile. "I'll see you later on tonight."

Jax shakes his hand with a nod. "I'll send you the address."

Johnathan lets go of Jax and extends his hand to me. "I look forward to getting to know you better over dinner."

"Should be fun," I squeak, shaking his hand. His touch is just as electric as I remember, and I quickly turn and walk away. My body follows Jax back to the car, but my mind is back in that hotel room. At least I know why he had to leave so suddenly.

"All right. Mission accomplished. Where do you want to go first?" Jax asks as he holds the passenger door open for me.

"I thought you were the tour guide," I muse and shake my umbrella on the sidewalk.

"Fine. I'll leave you in suspense until we get there."

He wasn't the only one. I look back out to the cemetery before closing the door.

I SIFT through the various boxes that cover my new room. The rain put a slight damper on the sightseeing, and I'm not too upset about it. After seeing Johnathan again, my mind can barely focus on anything else. Even if he's already seen me in my birthday suit, I still want to make the effort to look nice. I groan. Why didn't I better label these boxes?

Jax cracks the door open. "Everything okay?"

I lace my fingers behind my head and stare at the boxes. "Just trying to unpack. You'd think a girl with two degrees would know how to properly label things."

"Don't worry about that stuff right now. You have time to unpack and get your life together."

"But what about dinner?"

He leans on the doorframe. "Just wear something

from your suitcase. What about the dress from the wedding?"

"No," I balk. "I can't wear that again."

He cocks an eyebrow at me. "What happened to your dress?"

Other than the fact that Johnathan already tore it off me a few nights ago?

"It's dirty," I stutter. "Got clumsy with the wine and it's a whole thing to get the stain out. I'll just keep looking for something."

"Whatever." Jax shrugs. "We're leaving here in an hour, so you better be ready by then."

I give him a thumbs-up. "Got it."

He closes the door, and I fall back onto the bed. I'm running out of time. How is a girl supposed to focus when all she can think of is sex?

I TUG at the hem of my green dress as Jax and I stand in front of the restaurant. The wind whips around my ankles, and I shiver with the regret of not choosing something a little warmer. The price of beauty is overrated. At least the rain finally stopped. The lights of the different restaurants glow in the puddles on the sidewalk, and a group of girls walks past us. Must be nice to be so carefree. I shiver as the wind picks up again.

"Why can't we just wait inside?" I complain. "I'm freezing."

"He should be here any minute," Jax reassures me.

"I hope so," I mumble.

"Next time we go out, bring a jacket."

"Noted."

I shift uncomfortably as the wind continues to blow around us. The anticipation of seeing him again is making me lightheaded. *Keep your head, Kylie. Remember how to breathe.* The last thing I want is for Johnathan to find me passed out on the concrete.

A sleek, black car slows in front of us. My heart kicks into overdrive as Johnathan steps out of the back, a Secret Service–looking man holding the door open for him. His eyes search for me the moment he steps out the car. I feel like a fan girl at the edge of the red carpet as he walks toward us, a grin on his face as he strikes an exaggerated pose for Jax. Guess they are as close as Jax says.

"Look at Mr. Fancy Pants." Jax claps. "Hasn't even been twenty-four hours and you've already transformed into royalty."

"Believe me, it's not glamorous." Johnathan relaxes his goofy stance and looks at me. "Nice to see you again, Kylie."

I'm paralyzed by his gaze. The way he says my name sends a thrill of pleasure down my spine, and I politely nod. "Hi."

"I already made reservations, so we are good to go," Jax says, extending his hand toward the door.

Johnathan holds it open. "After you."

"Such a gentleman." Jax curtsies and walks inside.

I follow behind my brother, my mind racing. How am I supposed to get through dinner when I can't even think of anything to say back to him? Was that night at the wedding the last ounce of interesting I had left in me? My fingers accidentally brush Johnathan's side as I pass through the door, gliding against his crotch.

I snap my head up with wide eyes. "I'm so sorry."

"Don't be," he whispers, voice thick with desire. His scent overpowers me, and I want nothing more than to steal Johnathan away for the rest of the night.

"Kylie, I thought you were cold," Jax scolds me.

I tear my gaze from those lustful eyes and hurry faster inside. This is going to be impossible.

CHAPTER 9

Johnathan

SHE'S GORGEOUS. That green dress draws me in even more than the red one. Every swing of her hips has me hypnotized. Was her touch intentional? Her expression was shocked, but her fingers still lingered. I'm glad I was able to convince my new henchmen to wait outside the restaurant. The last thing I need is some lingering paparazzi to catch me lusting over Kylie. I follow them into the dimly lit waiting area, the low din of the dining room surrounding us as we walk to our table. I glance at the brick walls for a back exit. Maybe I can find a reason to get her alone. Pick up where we left off and then...

No. I need to calm down. Jax will murder me if he finds out that I banged his little sister. Of all the things, why did she have to be his sister? I should've known. I was at his cousin's wedding after all. Something should've given it away. But the more I watch those hips sway in front of me, the more I can't see a single similarity.

"All right, what do we have here?" Jax plops into his chair and scans the menu as I settle into my seat across from her.

Kylie. A fitting name for a dark beauty. Her eyes flit from me to her menu and back to me. She's just as flustered as I am. Does she want me just as badly?

The waitress snags my attention as she puts down a basket of breadsticks between us. "Can I get you guys anything to get started?"

"I'll have a lemonade," Kylie says, not bothering to look up from her menu.

"Rum and Coke for me." Jax nods.

The waiter stares at me expectantly. "And you, sir?"

"Um." I blink at my menu, the words looking like squiggles on the page. "I'll just have a water."

"Sounds good." She looks me once over before walking away, her hips swinging harder than before. She's cute, but Kylie beats her out by a mile. Not that it makes a difference with Jax sitting right next to me. Fate has been cruel to me these past few days.

"I take you out for dinner and you order a water." Jax slaps me on the arm. "Next you'll be ordering a cucumber side salad."

"Sorry." I laugh. "I'm just a bit distracted today."

"I bet," Kylie's voice pipes up from across the table. Jax snaps his head her way, and she glances between the both of us. "What? His dad just died. Cut him some slack."

"Yeah, but his dad had it coming." Jax leans back with ease. "No offense, man, but your dad was the angriest, most stressed-out guy I've ever met. Now that you're in charge, you can take your life back. Call the shots. Be the big wig shaking the hands of all those politicians your dad loved so much."

He has a point. With everything officially in my name, I'll be the one calling the shots at the daily meetings. Whether they like it or not, they answer to me. Including the viper queen. I imagine sitting in my dad's office as I throw divorce papers at Isabella, money raining down on me as I smoke a cigar. "If only it were that easy."

"Just lay down the law. Let everyone know that you're in charge and they'll have to accept it."

"It's not that. There's just so much to work out, I don't even know where to start." I steal a glance at Kylie, who continues to hide behind her menu.

Jax flips through his own menu, oblivious. "Didn't your dad have an assistant or a secretary?"

"That's rich." I laugh. "That man barely let anyone touch anything in that place. I was probably the closest thing he had to an assistant."

"Sounds like you need to hire a clone," Kylie chimes in, setting her menu aside.

I glance at her with a smirk. "If you find one, let me know."

"That's it!" Jax slams his fist on the table.

The waitress returns with our drinks and sets them down quickly. Her eyes are wide with surprise as she glances at Jax. "I'll give you guys a few more minutes."

"Please." Kylie smiles at her. The waitress nods, and Kylie elbows Jax in the side. "Will you calm down?"

"Yeah, Jax. You're scaring the staff." I pick up my glass, grateful for the water.

"I've just come up with the most brilliant plan and solution combo." Jax takes a sip of his rum, pausing for dramatic effect. "Kylie just moved here, and she's looking for a job. Plus, she's a beast when it comes to real estate. So what if Kylie was your assistant?"

I choke on my water, coughing loud enough to turn a few heads. Kylie? My assistant? The thought both terrifies and intrigues me. I glance at her, eyes wide and unmoving.

"Sorry." I wipe my mouth, clearing out the last of the water from my windpipe. "But I don't think that she would fit in at Ronsberry Law Firm. It's not the easiest job being the personal assistant to the CEO."

"Oh, come on." He pouts. "She is a perfect candidate. Who better to help you with beastly real estate transactions than the beast of real estate?"

"Please stop referring to your sister as a beast." She grimaces. "It's weird."

I rub my eyes, entertaining the thought. Jax isn't wrong. I could use someone to help me while I sort all of this out. I hate when Jax is right. Nothing good ever comes of it. But if she is as good as Jax says, I would have more time to sort through the fine print of my marriage agreement. Plus having her so close wouldn't be such a bad thing. Would it? But what do I do about Isabella? Jesus, it's been a while since I've completely forgotten she existed. What a welcomed turn of events. If only I can forget her entirely.

I steal a glance at Kylie. How would I even begin to explain to her that I'm married?

Kylie will definitely kill me. But she's going to find out either way at this point. And it's not like I'm in a real marriage. Maybe they have fake business arranged marriages where she comes from. As if. She stares at me from across the table, her silence growing by the minute.

I suck in a breath. "What do you say? Do you want to be my assistant?"

CHAPTER 10

Kylie

ME? An assistant? They have to be joking.

"No offense, guys, but I didn't just spend seven years in school just to end up as someone's assistant."

Even if I would be working for Johnathan, being an assistant is a big slap in the face. A girl has some standards. Especially after moving her whole life across the country.

"Everyone has to start somewhere, Kylie," Jax says. "And wouldn't you want to work for someone that you know rather than some random guy in a suit?"

A friendly face is one thing. But when all I can imagine is Johnathan bending me over his desk, I highly doubt that much work is going to get done.

"What am I even being offered? An assistant sounds like pennies compared to real estate."

He looks at me as if he was just presented with a challenge. "I'll pay you twice the going rate of what you're qualified for. For a starting position, of course. And if you decide to leave me, it will look good on your resume."

His slick smile seizes my heart, and I can't help but smile back. "Are you trying to bribe me?"

"Maybe." He shrugs. "I mean I'm sure that being new in town gives you plenty of connections to draw from. Or were you waiting for those big real estate agencies to just give you a call once you landed?"

He's baiting me. It isn't the worst offer in the world. Jax did say he was just promoted to CEO of Ronsberry Law Firm. Having a strong connection in this city could be just what I need to land an even bigger firm. A bigger plus would be seeing Johnathan every day and getting paid for it. Maybe things could get serious between us over time. Is it too farfetched an idea? Or are his social ranks too high for me to even be considered more than a quick fling on an island?

"Come on, Kylie," Jax pleads. "Just take the job. Or do you want me to go weeks with sleepless nights wondering what will become of my baby sister? I'll be left to wonder if you'll end up a real estate queen or unglamorous hooker. Oh, the agony."

"I promise to be a complete gentleman," Johnathan chimes in, holding his fingers up like a cub scout. "No funny business. After all, you're my good friend's sister."

Too late for those kinds of promises. But I guess I

don't really have much of a choice if my own brother thinks I'll end up a hooker otherwise. And it's not like I have anything lined up anyway. If I turn this down, the only thing I'll be doing Monday morning is job hunting.

"Fine," I cave. Challenge accepted. "But only until something better comes along."

"If it comes along." He winks at me.

My cheeks flame, and I cool my wandering thoughts with my lemonade. Jax holds out his glass in the middle of the table. "To new beginnings."

"To new beginnings," I cheer, clinking my glass against theirs.

Did I seriously just agree to being an assistant?

Jax looks around, fingers drumming against the table. "Where did our waitress go? I'm ready to order."

"I think you scared her away with your ideas." Johnathan laughs.

"Well, I'm going on a hunt for the bathroom." Jax looks my way. "If she does come back, tell her I want the Salmon Fresco."

"One salmon coming right up."

I do my best to act normal as he walks away. We're finally alone. I don't look at Johnathan, afraid he might see the lust lingering in my eyes. The last thing I want to come across as is desperate.

"So, should I start calling you boss now or after dinner?" I ask, gripping my menu.

"I think we should wait till the ink's dry before we start getting too formal."

I can feel his eyes on me but refuse to look up, the shrimp on the page staring back at me. "All right."

"Why don't you pass by the office tomorrow and we can sort everything out? I can show you around the place and we can get better acquainted."

My heart does a backflip, and I clear my throat. "Anything in particular you want me to wear?"

"Does it matter?"

I break my staring contest with the shrimp and meet his gaze, his teeth grazing his bottom lip. A tease through and through. Well, two can play at that game.

"I guess it all depends on how much of me you want?"

"More than I have right now." His eyes rake every inch of me, and I bite my own lip. Maybe I can get Jax drunk enough to send him back home alone in a cab. I'll charm Johnathan to take me back to his place and then...

"All ready to order?"

I look up and blink at the waitress. How long has she been standing there? I look around for Jax and sigh in relief when he's nowhere in sight.

"Yes, my friend will be having the Salmon Fresco," Johnathan says. "I'll have the Ravioli Special."

"What I miss?" Jax asks, plopping back in his chair between us.

"Not much." I shrug, glancing at my menu before ordering. I'm calm. There's nothing happening between me and Johnathan. Nothing at all.

"I'M TELLING YOU, he was flirting with you."

I click on the light of my room and toss my shoes in the corner. "Give it a rest, Jax."

"I'm serious," he slurs. "If he does something to you at work, you let me know. I'll come right down there."

"And do what? Take him out to another dinner?"

He pouts from the doorframe. "I'm just trying to make sure my baby sister is safe."

"Will you stop worrying?" I sigh. "I'm not some helpless little kid, you know."

"I know." He blows me a kiss. "Goodnight, Kylie."

"Goodnight."

The boxes surround me as I collapse back in my bed. The past few days replay in my mind like a movie. His scent faintly clings to the front of my dress from the hug he gave me before we left. Just the scent alone stirs my insides.

The sound of the TV in the other room is all the cue I need to turn off the lights and slide under the covers. No chance that Jax was coming to check on me in his drunken state. I know he can be protective, but I'm not a little kid anymore. I'm a woman. And my desires are strong.

My dress falls away, and I'm back in the hotel room with Johnathan. I twirl my fingers around my clit at the memories. Was he thinking about me tonight? Was he touching himself to the memories of being inside me? I can still see those hungry eyes of his from across the dinner table. Nothing on that menu was going to satisfy him. Only the taste of me. I twirl my fingers faster, back arching as I live in my memories.

Oh, Johnathan.

I lay back breathless and sink deeper under the covers. This morning I was a jobless newbie, and now I'm set to start my very first day with my one-night stand bright and early tomorrow. This is too unreal. But I'm not complaining. Not at all.

CHAPTER 11

Johnathan

Oh, how I loathe this place.

The rain slides down the windows that overlook Manhattan as I do my best to straighten out this mess of an office. Mounds of papers cover most of the place, including the long meeting table that sits dusty on the far side of the room. Various photos of my dad line the walls. No family. Not even a company photo. Just Dad shaking hands with whatever new politician or rich investor approached him that day. His smug face stares at me from across the room as I stand behind his desk. It's only eight in the morning, and I already crave something stronger than coffee.

The mahogany monument that my father spent most of his life behind is a sea of chaos. Nothing but unlabeled folders and a coffee mug full of old pens. How did he even get anything done? If anyone tries to break in and steal the family secrets, good luck to them. Not that they would get very far with the amount of security we have downstairs.

I glance at the clock hanging above the door, my palms sweaty as I set down yet another stack of papers by the window ledge. Kylie will be here in a few minutes. Just the thought of her brightens my day. When Jax first suggested her as my assistant, I thought it was another one of his sick jokes. But now that I'm here knee deep in papers, I can't help but count down the moments until she arrives. There're so many things that I have to teach her. If only I can get this place organized so I can think. Maybe the meeting table will be a better place to start.

My phone vibrates, and I manage to pluck it out of the mess in time, Isabella's name written across the screen. Speaking of messes.

"Well, this is a surprise," I answer. "Don't tell me that your credit cards have stopped working."

"Hilarious." Her tone is dry as usual, not even a hint of emotion sparking her tone. Did I marry a person or a robot?

I thumb through an overstuffed folder with a sigh. "What do you want, Isa? I'm busy."

"Is that anyway to talk to your wife?" she snaps. "I called to remind you about the charity dinner tonight. Your dad was supposed be the guest of honor. You're welcome."

Crap. That was today, wasn't it? I abandon the folder on the desk and shift the phone to my other ear. "I was thinking about canceling that appearance.

They should be more than understanding since their guest of honor is six feet under."

"What? No! You have to go!" she yells. I guess she's human after all.

"I don't have to do anything. I'm the CEO."

"Exactly. Johnathan, think of how weak you'll look to the competition if you don't attend. As the new CEO, it's your job to keep this company running and maintain its reputation."

She has a point. My dad always went out of his way to show up to every event he could. It was the main philosophy of his success. The more they see you, the more they fear you.

I lean back on the edge of the desk and watch the rain fall with disdain. I hate when she's right. "Fine, I'll go."

"Good. What time should I be ready?"

I nearly fall onto the floor. "I didn't realize you were invited."

"Well, how would it look if you showed up to such an important event without your wife? And at such a trying time. We both know you need all the support you can get. What a better way than leaning into sympathy?"

She's a snake and she knows it. I glance at the clock and panic sets in. Kylie will be here any second, and I still haven't written down her task list. How will it look if I'm unprepared for her? I was the one who offered the position after all. Whether I like it or not, Isabella has me cornered. "Fine. I'll have someone pick you up at five."

"Five thirty."

I open my mouth to correct her, but she's already gone. A scream bubbles in my throat, and I down the last bit of my morning coffee to calm my nerves. Great, now I have to play nice with a bunch of drunk, rich snobs later and pretend to miss my old man. And with Isabella on my arm. Of all people. The thought of receiving all of those condolences exhausts me. Was I really trapped into this life forever? The buzz of the intercom saves me from my thoughts, and I brush the sweat off my palms before pushing the button.

"Yes?"

"Mr. Ronsberry," Cindy crackles through the speaker. "Ms. Kylie has just arrived. She will be up in a moment to see you."

"Thank you, Cindy."

The speaker goes dead, and I can't help but give into the excitement coursing through me. Now is not the time for Isabella and her dinner plans. For now, everything is about getting the new girl up to speed.

My old desk stares at me from the corner, the small vase of fresh flowers I placed next to the desktop the only bright thing in the room. My henchmen didn't even question why I wouldn't give my assistant her own office, and I'm grateful. The less people questioning me the better. I hope Kylie doesn't find it too forward of me to have her so close. I've tried to convince myself that it's because of my undeniable attraction for her. But I know deep down it's because I'm terrified of being alone in this office. It's as if my dad's ghost is going to pop out at any moment and tell me how bad of a job I'm doing. I glance back at the piles of papers with a heavy sigh. Isabella wasn't wrong about keeping appearances. Messy or not, this office has to get back up and running today. Thank God Kylie is on her way up to help. I don't think that I can do this without her.

CHAPTER 12

Kylie

I SMILE at the lady behind the desk as she hands me my brand-new badge, the Ronsberry Law Firm emblem freshly printed above my name.

"Take the elevators on the left and head up to the fortieth floor," she instructs, pointing down the hall.

"Thanks." I nod, my heels echoing as I cross through the lobby. The guards nod at me as I pass, their eyes cold and uninviting. Johnathan wasn't kidding. This place is intense. But so am I.

An elevator opens, and I stand aside as a group of men step out. They don't even notice me as they talk amongst themselves, and I slide into the elevator before it closes. At least I'll have a minute to myself before I see him. The thought alone makes me blush, and I grip the handle of my soggy umbrella tighter. It's no big deal. I'm just on my way up to see my new boss. Every flight I climb brings me closer to him, and the butterflies in my stomach won't quit.

My brother's accusations from last night echo in the back of my mind, deepening my blush. I need to get a grip. Today is all about business. No matter what happens, I have to keep my cool.

The elevator doors open, and I step into long hallway lined with offices. Nothing but men in suites either talking to clients or glued to their screens. How am I supposed to find Johnathan in this place? I wander around with my head held high. It's not like I don't belong here. I'm a member of this company just like the rest of them. Even if I am a bit lost.

A huge, wooden door at the far end of the hall sticks out from the others, and I slink closer. The handles are gold with the letters "F R" engraved on the front, the ghost of a plaque in the middle of the door. There's no doubt about it. But just to be sure, I knock on the door with authority.

"Come in."

His voice sends my heart into a frenzy, and I grip the handle. *Calm down, Kylie. Don't let him see you sweat on the first day.*

He stands in front of a massive desk covered in papers. The more I look around, the more I can't help but think of those hoarder shows my mom watches on TV. Is this really the CEO's office?

"You made it." Johnathan smiles at me, extending his hand.

I step into the room and firmly shake his hand. "Did you really expect me not to show?"

"I was hoping I'd have more time to organize."

His hand lingers on mine for a while, and part of me hopes that he brings me closer. I wouldn't mind being in his arms again. Especially the way he looks in that suit.

I let my hand fall and take a step back, fully taking in the place. "Your dad sure left a mess."

"Oh, don't worry about all of this." He waves a hand. "I've come prepared."

He leads me away from the mess to a lone desk in the corner. Not as massive as his, but good enough. I hang my purse off the back of the chair and notice the small "welcome" sign sticking out of the flowers. A gentleman through and through.

"Since today is my first day as well, I thought we could get you familiar with what goes on here at Ronsberry." He leans over, his arm brushing against mine as he starts typing on the keyboard. I swallow hard as he continues. "I've had HR set up your email and company profile."

"Great," I say, voice neutral. It's all I can do to focus as he guides me through a tour of the tools I'll be using. It's all so straightforward and organized. I can't help but glance back at the papers behind us. "So, if you guys have such a tight system, what is all of that?"

"That," he sighs, standing back up, "is my father's life work. He liked to keep things old school, so the most important files are, well, somewhere in that mess."

"Any chance you need a hand sorting it out?" I look up at him. "I'm a pretty good organizer."

He turns toward me, his body inches from mine. "Where would you suggest we start?"

His eyes trail down past my face and back up to meet my gaze once more. How am I supposed to focus when he looks at me like that? And here I thought I dressed pretty modestly today.

"How much time do you have?" I breathe. *Focus, Kylie. Don't drop your guard.*

The question seems to bring him back to his senses, and he looks back at the computer. A calendar pops up on the desktop. I hover over his shoulder as he scrolls through various meetings and calls.

"Shit," he mumbles. I guess cleaning will have to wait.

"Leaving me alone on my first day," I muse. "Boss of the year."

He shakes his head. "I'm sorry. I promise that after this week, I'll have a better handle of things."

"You better."

Johnathan's eyes quickly search mine in a panic. "I really am sorry."

"I'm kidding." I chuckle, and he seems to relax at my playful mood. Was he always this on edge? I settle into my desk as he crosses back toward the window and grabs his bag off his chair.

"I'll see you later." He waves as he walks toward the door.

"Good luck." I wave back. With the way that this place runs, it looks like he is going to need it.

The loud thud of the door confirms I'm alone, and I slump in my chair with a sigh. Not even ten minutes with him and I nearly lost my mind. Am I so deprived of his touch that I'm willing to do it in this wreck of an office? I scroll through the calendar. According to this, Johnathan will be gone for hours. I look back at the mess and can't help but check it out. Mounds of folders and papers litter the table. There is no way that Johnathan will be able to think straight in this mess. It's not like he said I can't help. I shrug off my jacket and toss it across the back of a chair. It may not be real estate, but this is my job now. And, boy, is there work to be done.

CHAPTER 13

Johnathan

IF ANOTHER PERSON asks me how I'm doing, I might jump out the window.

My mind buzzes with the babble of various meetings with clients and buyers, each one expressing in detail their sympathies. Once I get back to that office, I'm going to have to change my schedule around. If I can manage to find the computer in that mess. Maybe I'll just use my old one to save time. I grip the golden handle, the sound of rustling papers coming from the other side of the door. Has my dad come back from the dead to collect a few things?

The smell of mustard hangs in the air as I walk into an empty desk. My heart sinks. Were we robbed?

"Surprise!"

I yelp loudly as Kylie cheers from her desk in the corner. The blur of meetings felt so normal that I forgot she was even here. But oh how glad I am that she is. Her jacket is gone, her once neat bun slightly wilted. She tucks a few stray strands behind her ear. "So, what do you think?"

I scan the room a second time. The cluttered disaster I started my day with now sits neatly stacked and cleaned. In a matter of hours, she managed to do all of this? My eyes fall on a brown leather sofa near the window.

"Where did that come from?" I ask, walking toward it.

"It was under all those papers." Kylie sighs. "Your dad sure had a weird system."

I look back at her. "That mess had a system?"

"Apparently." She motions over to the conference table across the room. "I ordered you lunch based on what was in the calendar. I figured you hadn't eaten, so I set it up for you."

I follow the scent of mustard and can't help but laugh out loud as I notice the overstuffed sub in the distance. Kylie's face creases with concern. "Did I do something wrong?"

"No." I laugh, wiping my eyes of a few tears. "Not at all. That lunch order used to be my dad's. I guess I was so used to seeing it, forgot to delete it from the system."

"Oh." Her voice is small. "I'm sorry."

"Don't be." I smile, the weight of the day lifted. "This is just the kind of thing I need after the last few hours I've had."

Her face brightens a little, and she nods. "Okay, good."

I take in her tired expression and motion her over to follow me. "Come split this with me. There's no way I can finish this thing all by myself."

"Oh, I'm not hungry." No sooner does she say it than her stomach grumbles in protest. Her cheeks flame and she slowly stands. "I guess I could take a little break."

Her heels are muted by the carpet as she crosses to join me at the conference table. I can't even remember the last time they even used this thing. Once a dusty relic now shined in the afternoon glow. And it's all thanks to Kylie.

I hold out the corner chair for her, and she sits with a mumble of thanks.

I make myself comfortable at the head chair, the massive sandwich sitting in front of me. The sight of it is less appealing up close. I guess I know what caused my dad's heart attack. After a few tries, I manage to break the monstrosity in half and place it in front of Kylie on a napkin.

"Thanks." Her hands look so small as she wraps them around the monster sub, and we eat in silence.

It's been a while since I've shared a meal with someone. Normally it's a quick bite of takeout in my office before my next meeting. But something about sitting next to Kylie seems different. Almost like I can sit here with her forever. I know it won't last. So

I steal a silent glance her way and relish in the moment before it's gone.

"OH, JOHNATHAN!"

I refrain from rolling my eyes and force another tightlipped smile as another drunken woman runs up to me with tears in her eyes. This is the fourth woman tonight that has run up to me, and it doesn't seem like she will be the last. Isabella stands at my side, hugging the woman. "Oh, it's all right. Frank is in a better place now. Don't you worry, Mrs. Curtis. Ronsberry Law Firm is as strong as ever."

For once I'm grateful to have her here. How she manages to remember all these names is beyond me. What, did she study the guestlist before she got here? And that smile. You would think that she is a nun at a charity event the way she speaks to this distraught woman. This isn't the same pill of a woman that stood next to me at the cemetery. This is the people's famous Saint Isabella.

Mrs. Curtis extends her hands out to me, and I take them as she sniffles. "Johnathan, your father was such a great man. If there is anything you need, please, just let me know."

"Thank you, Mrs. Curtis. I'll be sure to do that."

She squeezes my hands one final time before drifting back to the bar. What I wouldn't give to have a drink. Isabella wraps her arm around mine and leads me away.

"Take me to the bathroom right now," she hisses in my ear. "That disgusting woman got her tears on me."

So much for being a saint.

I numbly lead her through the double doors and down the hall. The noise and chaos of the dinner falls away, and I'm grateful. One more sobbing drunk and I'd have lost my shit.

"When we go back in there, I'm grabbing a drink," I tell Isabella as she lets go of me.

She rests her hand on the bathroom door and looks back, that pageant smile gone. "One drink to be polite."

There's the wife I loathe. I collapse into a nearby bench and check my phone as she disappears to go polish her horns. Only a few more hours and I'll be released from this torture. I wonder what Kylie's doing right now. Probably at home with Jax without a care in the world. Would it be too weird to pass by? I can already see Kylie opening up the door. She'll be wearing something casual. Nothing more than a t-shirt. I'm sure they wouldn't mind if I—

"All right," Isabella declares as she emerges from the bathroom. "Let's finish this up so I can go home. My feet are starting to swell."

"Maybe wearing flats will brighten your mood."

"Bite me, Johnathan." She holds out her arm with pursed lips.

I groan and stuff my phone in my pocket. Do I really have to drag her back out into that booze-smelling room? Maybe a bit of charm will release me early.

I lace my arms with hers and cup my free hand under her chin. "Don't you think we've done enough for tonight? Why don't we just sneak out of here and go home? I'll even stop by that place you like on the way."

She shakes free of my touch and brushes herself off, disgusted. "Absolutely not. What is with you? Has being CEO made you forget our arrangement?"

I clear my throat and adjust the knot on my tie. "No. It hasn't."

"I'm going in there to see if I can snag us a few more benefactors. You go get that drink and fix whatever has come over you. I'll find you if I need you."

She stomps away, her modest attire only highlighting the features she lacks. I guess that adds to her sainthood act. But I know better. Tomorrow I'm canceling all meetings, image be damned. I need to get out of this marriage. And nothing's going to hold me back from trying.

CHAPTER 14

Kylie

I WALK DOWN the hall with more confidence than
ever. Living in the city is more exciting than I'd ever
imagine it would be. Last night, Jax prepared a
massive congratulatory dinner for completing my
first day of work. I guess even overprotective big
brothers have their perks now and then. I nearly
chugged my weight in wine in celebration; I'm
surprised I'm not clinging to the wall with a hang-
over. The only thing that would've made the night
better was if Johnathan had stopped by. Not that I
told my brother that. Knowing him, he'd have me
shipped back home if he even caught a whiff of how
I felt about his friend. Leave it to those big brother
instincts to dampen a harmless crush.

After all, that's all this is. Isn't it? Nothing more
has been shared between us but an extra-large sandwich. Well, since I got here anyway. My cheeks heat
up, and I blush at the thought of my accidental touch

at the restaurant. No, stop it. There's not time for that. A guy from one of the offices looks up at me, and I wave as I walk past.

After yesterday's massive cleaning spree, I feel like I've earned my right to be here. Not that anyone else would understand. It's not every day you have to clean up the ghost of Frank Ronsberry.

"Fuck!"

Johnathan's voice echoes through the entire floor, and I quicken my pace. A turn of the golden knob and I'm almost hit square in the face with a manilla folder.

"Shit!" Johnathan yelps. "Kylie. I'm so sorry. Please, come in."

I shuffle a few stray papers at my feet over the threshold and close the door behind me. My heart sinks as I look around the office, papers and folders thrown around Johnathan in a new kind of chaos.

"What happened?"

"I've been up all night looking for something. An agreement," Johnathan mumbles, sipping his coffee with a shaky hand as he squints at the papers gripped in the other. His usual demeanor has been replaced with a wild-eyed man in half a tuxedo. This was not the same Johnathan I left yesterday.

I cross through the mess toward my desk. "Are you okay?"

"Ha!" He laughs, a crazed look in his eye as he glances at me. "I'm doing fantastic."

"Johnathan."

He looks around the room and back at me, scratching his head. "I'm sorry. I know how hard you worked on this yesterday. And I just—"

"I don't care about the mess," I snap. "I care about what the fuck is going on with you."

He blinks at me. "I'm—"

"Not fine," I finish. "Look, I'm here if you want me as your assistant. But if this going to work, you're going to have to trust me with a little more than your schedule."

He stares at me, those lost swirls softening a bit. "You're right." He sighs, collapsing back into the sofa. He pats the cushion beside him with a heavy hand. "Come here. Someone other than me might as well know the truth."

The truth? I abandon my purse on my desk and make my way over to him. He rubs his eyes as I make myself comfortable on the cold leather cushions. Has his father's death finally sunk in? Maybe this is what Jax had meant by freaking out.

"Now what I'm about to tell you is strictly confidential," Johnathan says. "Not even Jax can know about this."

My heart flutters a little, and I nod. "You have my word."

His hand falls from his eyes, and he looks at me. Even in his tired state he's still as handsome as ever.

"When I talked to my dad before he died," he starts, "he told me to keep safe. Something that he agreed to with Leonardo had him scared, but he died before he could tell me. I thought that I'd be able figure out what they agreed to, but so far, I haven't found shit."

I have no idea who Leonardo is, but the concern in Johnathan's face explains enough. "Why didn't you tell me yesterday? I could've helped—"

"I didn't want you involved in any of this." His eyes are sad yet sincere. "And I still don't. Let's just say Leonardo doesn't have the best reputation. He's been known to some as a very dangerous man, so whatever my dad was talking about has the potential to be a dangerous situation."

"Oh, and you expected to find what you're looking for with this kind of strategy?" I motion to the room. "Face it, you need my help."

He shakes his head. "I won't put my good friend's kid sister in danger."

"I'm not a little kid," I fume. "Especially when it involves my work."

Johnathan groans, internally at war as he looks away. Even this angry he's as handsome as ever. I gently rest my hand on his. He squeezes it tightly, his thumb rubbing over my knuckles. Even in such a crazed state his touch is gentle. Every motion sends sparks through me as he continues to gaze out the window.

"I don't want anything happening to you," he says, voice low. "If you got hurt, I could never forgive myself."

"Hey," I say, squeezing his hand a little. "I'll be

fine. There's a way for this work. But only if you want my help."

He shakes his head, finally turning back to me. "I'm not used to trusting other people. It never goes well."

"Well, I'm not people, am I?"

"No." He smirks a little. "You're definitely not."

Jax would kill me if he found out I was begging to be led into whatever danger lurks behind this agreement. But there is no way I am leaving Johnathan alone in this mess. This is bigger than some temp job, and I want to help any way that I can.

Johnathan sighs. "Looks like I'm out of options." His eyes are clear but weary as he takes both of my hands in his. "Kylie, will you please help me?"

I suppress the giggle of excitement bubbling in my throat and nod a little. "Where do you want us to start?"

CHAPTER 15

Johnathan

I WANT to tell her everything. But the more I say, the more at risk I am of her finding out about Isabella. I know she'll find out eventually, but why piss off the only ally I have in my corner? Especially when it's someone as brilliant as Kylie. I manage to clean up the mess I made in my tantrum and leave her in charge of thumbing through the rest. As much as I want to clear my schedule indefinitely, there's no way that every one of my dad's partners are sympathetic to his death. Life still must go on, and time is money in our line of work.

"Don't worry." Kylie smiled at me from her desk. "I've got your back."

That was days ago. With a week full of meetings and conference calls, I barely have time to do anything but eat, sleep, and shower. Popping into the office throughout the day just never seems to make it on the list. It's almost like I'm back to the old routine. Carrying the load of two people with ninety-nine percent less yelling. The only real difference is Kylie. Knowing that she's the one waiting for me on the other side of that door brings a sense of comfort to my day. My secret helper disguised as an assistant. If only I can make more time to check in on her and see what she's found. If anything at all.

I stifle a yawn and shuffle my way toward the elevator. The other offices sit dark around me. No surprise there. Even I shouldn't be here this late. I glance at my office in the distance and notice the light peeking out from under the door. There's no way she could still be here. But there's no harm in checking.

The creak of the office door seems so loud at night. Dim light from the table lamp casts a shadow over Kylie's face. She sits at the conference table, folders laid out around her like a barrier as she leans on one hand while she reads. I stand there frozen, captured by the sight of her. Even in the shadows she looks beautiful. Her eyes glance up from the folder open in front of her and she jumps at the sight of me.

"Sorry. I didn't mean to startle you." I guide the door closed before crossing over to her.

"No, it's fine." She relaxes. "I just got lost in deciphering this. Must've lost track of time."

"Anything good?" I ask, leaning over her shoulder.

"Define good."

Her scent soothes me as I read my dad's scribbled handwriting. I look past the open folder to the others, each one with a brightly colored sticky note on top.

"Fraud. Theft. Confused," I read aloud, picking one up. "What is all this?"

"That's what I've been trying to figure out." Kylie sighs. "None of this makes sense. Like this here." She flips through a few papers and holds them out to me. "There's a signed contract for construction on a new building, but nowhere in any of these folders does it go further than that. It's like they gave up building it before they even started."

"Plans fall through sometimes." I shrug, skimming the text.

"I thought so too. Until I found this signed renovation deal for a building down on 4th Street. When I did a quick search online, the building doesn't exist. It's a community garden."

My heart races, and I take the paper from her hands. The address written down is clearly typed. "Maybe someone just typed a number wrong?"

"I tried typing in different variations, but nothing comes up. This building just doesn't exist."

My mind tries to put it all together, but even more questions surface. Was this what my dad was trying to warn me about? But what does it mean? I look down at Kylie, my questions dissipating the moment I look into her eyes. So confident and determined to solve this mystery. Not a hint of fear or doubt. But at what cost? Nothing about this seems like the kind of work she should be doing at this hour. Especially if Isabella finds us like this. I can already hear the screams of outrage and shudder at the thought.

"We should call it a night, don't you think?" I rest a hand on her shoulder. "Your brother might get worried if you're out too late."

She shrugs me off. "My brother's worries are not my concern."

"They should at least be considered." I smirk.

"Look, you can go if you'd like," she snaps. "But I'm not leaving until I finish this folder."

Her fingers drum against the table, and she looks back at me with a sour expression.

Even at this late hour, she's still ready to keep going. A fiery woman through and through. And who am I to stop her?

I shrug off my jacket and drape it over the chair beside her. "Well, I'm definitely not going to leave you here by yourself. Especially if there's fraud involved."

Her gaze has changed from angry to curious. "You're not going to force me to leave?"

"Why would I dose out the fire of a spirit ready to help me with this case?" I loosen my tie and unbutton the cuffs of my shirt. "Feel free to get comfortable. I like to work in strange positions, so get ready for them."

"I don't think it'll be anything I can't handle." She winks at me.

My heart does a backflip, and I look her once over. The office seems less ominous in the night. A different kind of energy fills the air, whispering with possibility. No ghosts threatening to make an appearance. The office at night belongs to me and Kylie. My fingers are still alive with her touch, and I want more. No, stop it. How will it look if I start making a move after suggesting that we stay and work? The last thing I need is Jax banging down my door with accusations of being a perverted asshole.

"Okay then." I laugh nervously. "I guess I better order us some fuel. No use decoding on an empty stomach."

"Good thinking." Kylie nods, turning back to the folders.

I turn to hide my growing desires, and I grab my phone with a sigh. I guess late night Chinese will have to be comfort enough.

CHAPTER 16

Kylie

I LEAN on Johnathan's shoulder as I crack open another folder. This is the fourth one in the last hour that I've gone through and still no connection to the missing properties. I glance up at Johnathan, his brow creased with concentration as he compares two documents side by side. The past few weeks have finally broken the awkward, sexual spell between us as we've poured over every document left behind by Frank Ronsberry together, and I'm grateful. For a second I thought I was doomed to fidget around Johnathan for the rest of my life. At least until I get another taste of him. But all of that is behind me now. With all of these late-night meetings I can barely keep my eyes open, never mind think of sex.

"Are there any eggrolls left?" I ask, sitting up from my slouched position.

"You ate the last one half an hour ago," Johnathan responds without looking up.

"We're going to have to figure out something else to eat soon," I muse, snagging a bag of crunchy noodles. "A girl can't only live off of lo mien."

He peers over his papers with an amused expression. "Are we being picky about our midnight snacks?"

"All I'm saying is that for a city that never sleeps, I'm not seeing much of a variety around here."

"Well, remind me to bust out the caviar next time."

His smile is infectious. How can he still have so much energy after the past two weeks? If I was working with anyone else, I'd probably hate everything about this. But sitting next to him almost feels like I'm doing a research paper with a friend. Except that this friend is a really hot billionaire who also happens to be my boss. Yup, totally normal.

I rise to stretch with a yawn, and I can feel his eyes on me.

"Want to call it a night?" he asks. "I'll have my men pull a car out front for you."

"Sure." I sigh, adjusting my shirt back into place. "I'll go grab my things."

He's become used to the roll. I think. The way he gives orders these days seems surer than the man that hired me. The ghost of his father still lingers, no doubt. But the way he directs his men has the weight of authority of a true leader. I wouldn't mind if he laid down the law on me once in a while. I can already see the scandal.

"Kylie?"

His voice snaps me out of my thoughts. "Hm?"

I turn to find Johnathan already by the door. "Ready to go?"

"Yeah, sorry." I shrug on my jacket and hike my purse on my shoulder as I quickly cross the room.

He holds the door open for me with a smirk. "Don't start burning out on me."

"Wouldn't dream of it." I try to squeeze past him, but he holds his arm out in front of me.

I look up at him to see his face creased with concern. "I'm serious. If this become too much, just say the word and we'll slow down."

I'm lost in his sincerity. With the way he started this quest, I thought he would be more of a tyrant. But the way he looks at me makes it seem like we have all the time in the world.

"Shall we?" He drops his hand, and I scurry out the door.

I can feel the heat on my cheeks, and I do my best to calm myself before Johnathan notices. My fingers go to hit the down button but meet his instead. The casual feeling between us is gone, that familiar zing of electricity running through me as I recoil my hand.

"Sorry," I mumble, staring down the doors. I just have to keep it together long enough to get in the car. Why did he have to say all of those things?

Those sweet, wonderful things? The elevator arrives, and I do my best to calmly walk on, hands to myself to avoid any more of his electric touch. The last time we were like this together, he nearly took all of me before we even left the lobby. Now I find myself standing on the opposite side of the elevator for reassurance. His eyes are on me again, but different than before. I look down at my phone, trying to look busy. He inches closer, but I refuse to look at him. Just a few flights more and I'll be safe from temptation.

"Kylie," he breathes.

The way he says my name convinces me I'm safe. I steal a glance and know instantly I've made a mistake. His eyes are no longer clear; those lustful clouds are back and tempting. Maybe it's the burnout setting in, but I inch closer to him. A single kiss won't hurt. I'm pretty sure there's a place out there that kisses their bosses on the lips as a sign of goodbye. Right? Maybe even more than once?

The elevator doors swing open, and I jump back, half expecting someone to be there. But only the dark lobby greets us as Johnathan stands up straight and holds out his arm once more. The gentleman has returned.

"After you."

I refrain from running all the way to the car, and we cross the lobby together in silence. I want him. If I didn't live with overprotective Jax, I'd steal him away in a heartbeat. The cool night air sends a chill down my spine, and I do my best to avoid any more physical contact as I slide in the backseat.

"Goodnight." I smile, looking up at him. Every part of me wants to drag him in here by his tie and show him all the wild thoughts locked inside my head. His eyes search mine, and I'm convinced he can read my thoughts.

"Goodnight," he says, voice thick with desire as he closes the door between us.

I slump back in my seat and stare at him through the tinted glass. And here I thought we were making progress.

THE APARTMENT IS dark when I walk in, and I do my best to close the door without a sound. I guess Jax isn't the hard worker I thought he was. A light clicks on in the hallway, and Jax stands there in a blue robe and slippers.

"Do you have any idea what time it is?" he says.

I stand corrected. "I know. I'm sorry. I'll be quieter coming in."

"No, Kylie." He crosses his arms. "This is the third week in a row that you've been out late. At first, I was thinking that it's because you're in a new job. That you and Johnathan must be going over things. Business things. But now, I'm starting to think something else."

"Oh, will you give it a rest?" I yawn, grateful for

the shadows as I kick off my shoes. "There's nothing going on between me and your college BFF."

"Then why are you coming home at three in the morning?"

"I think your lawyer brain and your brother brain are starting to clash. Johnathan just has me on this special project. And as his personal assistant, it's my job to be thorough."

"That sounds like code for sex. Just admit it." He shakes his head, raking his fingers through his hair. "I really did expect more from Johnathan."

I can tell he's spiraling, and I'm too tired to argue. How do you outsmart a lawyer that knows you inside and out?

"Jax," I sigh. "It's late. Can we do this in the morning?"

"No, we can't." He walks toward me. "You are going to tell me everything now."

"Most people talk about their day over breakfast."

"Most people don't hide secrets." Jax takes out a crumbled sticky note from his robe pocket and holds it out to me. My own handwritten note with the word fraud stares back at me, and I take it with a sigh. He holds my face in his hands and looks me in the eye. "What does he have you roped into?"

I sit on the couch, nervously fidgeting with the cup of hot chocolate Jax handed me, before I spill every last detail of the past few weeks. Minus the sexual tension and the night at the wedding, Jax is caught up to speed. Not that I know much in the first place. Two weeks of research and I seem to still have more questions than answers.

"So, let me get this straight," Jax says, fuming. "Johnathan's late dad may have been involved in embezzlement and fraud, and you just agreed to help him look into it?"

"Well, yeah. What was I supposed to do?" I snap. "He's my boss, Jax. Regardless of your personal history, I've got a real chance to make a difference."

"Not if you end up in jail. Or dead!"

"You're being dramatic."

"Am I?" His tone is dark, eyes haunted. "Kylie, I've been working in this city for a while. I've seen some things. Things I hope you never get to see. And I have a feeling that this case, if you even want to call it that, leads to nowhere good."

"It can't be as bad as it sounds. We haven't even uncovered anything yet. It might actually be nothing."

"But it could still be something. And how is he supposed to protect you if he ends up going to jail for being Frank's right-hand man? I'm telling you, Kylie—"

"You can tell me whatever you want, but I'm not backing down from this."

He stares me down, lips turned down in a scowl. I abandon my mug on the coffee table and scoot closer to him. "Jax, I get that you don't like it. But you have to trust me on this."

"I want to." He sighs. "But this isn't something

you wait out and see what happens. I think you should figure a way out of this."

"Is this why you wanted me to live with you? So I can be under your big brother rule? If I wanted to be under someone's thumb, I would've stayed home with Mom and Dad."

I don't bother to wait for his response and make my way to my room, slamming the door for good measure. Dangerous or not, Johnathan is expecting me to help him. And I'm not about to let him down. Even if it means pissing off my brother in the process.

CHAPTER 17

Johnathan

I SIT at the conference table, eyes flicking from my list of clients to Kylie. She sits at the opposite end surrounded by papers and open folders, mumbling with a scowl on her face. Is she upset about the way I came across in the elevator? Did I misread her body language and the lure of her eyes?

"So I heard this pizza place is open late," I start. "Maybe we can try them tonight?"

Her head snaps my way, nothing but fear in her eyes. "Don't you think what we're doing is a little too dangerous for pizza?"

"Dangerous?" I blink at her. "Kylie, we haven't even found anything yet."

"But we could. You said it yourself that this could be dangerous. That this Leo guy was bad news."

"Well, did you find something that supports that?"

"No, but." She stands from her chair with a loud

groan and walks over to the window, arms crossed in front of her. She looks so small and afraid. This isn't the same Kylie that was fired up with determination. Is what she found so bad that she doesn't even want to tell me? I slide back from my work and move toward her. No use in prolonging the inevitable.

The night stretches below us, a glitter of orange lights amidst the shadows. It's the kind of view that people kill for. Something Leo has probably had his eye on from the moment he first walked through the door. I know the rumors painted him as an evil guy, but was he really dark enough to kill?

"The city sure looks beautiful at night," I say, clasping my hands behind my back. "You'd never know there was anything going on from up here."

"Jax says that there's always something happening in the city," Kylie spits, eyes glued to the street below.

"He's not wrong. Danger in the city is everywhere. Whether you see it or not."

"How can you be so calm?" Her eyes search mine, pleading to understand. "You're not scared that your dad might've involved you in something terrible?"

"But that's the thing, Kylie. I am scared." I chuckle sadly. "I'm terrified that whatever was haunting my dad might be haunting me." I take her small hands in mine and trace my thumbs over the backs of her knuckles. "I promise. I will never let anything bad happen to you."

"But what am I supposed to do if you go to jail? Or die? Or—"

My lips quickly silence her. As I cherish those thick lips pressing lightly against mine, it begins to stir the beast inside me. I cup her cheeks with my hands to bring her closer. I don't know what has gotten into me, but I don't want to lose her. I can feel my body aching for her; how can I get her to understand how much I need her to stay? I caress her with my lips, each kiss deeper than the last. She leans into me, a low moan escaping her throat. I feel her hands press into my chest, and she pulls away.

"Johnathan," she breathes, voice ragged.

I don't let go of her as I search her eyes. "I want you, Kylie. And I haven't wanted anything in a really long time."

"But why me?" she asks.

"Why not you?" I graze my tongue on her bottom lip and slide my hands down to her hips. I grip her ass hard as her tongue brushes against mine. Her taste is addicting. She leans back into the window ledge, and I press all of myself against her. Those hands that once pulled me away are now entangled in my hair, every stroke of those small hands encouraging me forward. My cock twitches with anticipation. I want her more than I ever have. I slide my hands under her shirt and fumble with the clasp. There's no one to hold us back. She'll be all mine once more.

The buzz of the phone vaguely registers as I trail

my kisses down her neck. Whoever is trying to get a hold of me will have to wait until later. The buzzing stops as I get the clasp undone. Finally.

The ring of the office phone rings loud in the silence, and Kylie pushes me away, eyes still laced with lust. We stare at each other as the phone continues to chime, each one sobering us up a little bit more. The ringing finally stops, but the moment is gone. I let go of my hold on her with a sigh and look out the window in an attempt to calm myself. "I'll go ahead and order that pizza."

"Sounds good," she squeaks, clearing her throat as she backs away from me. "I'm going to go wash my hands. For the, um, pizza."

I'm surprised she doesn't run out of the room, and I fall back into the overstuffed armchair as soon as the door slams closed. What is wrong with me? One minute I'm worried about her leaving and the next thing I know I'm a few motions away from sliding inside of her.

I let out a loud groan of frustration. Every minute she's in this office, the chemistry between us intensifies. Part of me wants to let a quick one out right here. No doubt Kylie was coming back any time soon. No. I have to keep my cool.

I grab my phone to place the pizza order. I wonder if Kylie likes sausage or pepperoni? I swipe open the screen, and the first thing I see is Isabella's name popping up as a missed call. That would explain the back-to-back phone calls. Wicked woman. She would be the one to interrupt me while I'm enjoying myself. As if being chained to her isn't enough misery. I click her name and pray for it to go to voicemail.

"I need to talk to you," she answers on the second ring, her voice extinguishing any lingering feelings of Kylie.

"I figured that's why you called," I grumble.

"Not now. Tomorrow."

I lean back in my chair, growing more irritated by the second. "Then why bother calling today? Next time, just send a text."

"Texting always leaves room for subliminal interpretation. Besides, I'm passing by the office tomorrow, and I want to make sure you'll be there. I need us to meet up early enough that my day won't be interrupted."

"Oh, we wouldn't want that," I mumble.

"What was that?"

"Nothing. Sounds good. I'll be here, as usual."

"You better be," she snaps. "I'll be there around seven. And don't keep me waiting."

She hangs up, and I'm tempted to hurl my phone across the room. The stacks of folders on the conference table seem to mock me with every passing day. Somewhere in this room is my ticket to freedom, and I'm no closer to finding it than I was a few weeks ago. I rub my eyes in frustration, the ghost of Kylie's lips still on mine. Am I really trapped in this life forever?

CHAPTER 18

Kylie

HE KISSED ME. Is this a dream?

I lean on the marble countertop and remind myself how to breathe. My brother's fear has all but consumed me these last few days, but all of it faded away with that one kiss. I still feel the wetness of his lips on mine. The feel of his hands on my back as he unclasped my bra. I'm glad it's the middle of the night; otherwise I'd be forced to compose myself in a cramped stall. I fling off my shirt and readjust my bra. Why did that phone have to ring?

One glance at my reflection gives away my lingering excitement. Flushed cheeks, a quivering smile, and a twisted bra. How obvious can I possibly be? There's no way that I can go back in there after that kiss and focus. Maybe I can pretend that I have a stomach bug and tell him that I need to leave now. I'm sure big brother Jax will be happy to see me home early. Every time I walk through door, it's nothing but a bombardment of questions. What did I find out about the case? Is there anything new? I'm surprised he doesn't have a voice recorder pressed to my face the way he wants information. Not that I've discovered much else besides phantom buildings and lost paper trails. Whatever Frank wanted to keep hidden, he did a fantastic job of doing it.

I splash some water on my cheeks to cool my blush and straighten up in the mirror. I'll just tell Johnathan that I'd like to go home early. It's not like he can tell me no. Right?

I slide my shirt back on and step back out into the empty hallway. The murmurs of Johnathan float down the hall, his tone all business. Was he seriously ordering a pizza after our make-out session? My steps are muted on the carpet, and I hover outside the door, trying to catch any hint of the conversation. By the time I lean into the door, Johnathan is silent and I'm left listening to my own hammering heartbeat. Looks like a good time as any to go back in there. I suck in a deep breath before opening the door, steeling myself for whatever wrath is about to come my way.

He stands by the conference table with a folder in his hand. *Just spit it out, Kylie.*

"Hey," Johnathan says before I can start. "I was thinking that we call it quits a little early tonight. I'm not feeling much like myself."

Well, that's an understatement. I guess he wasn't ordering a pizza after all. But then who was he talking to? And why the sudden change in attitude? Was it because I left in such a rush? What was I supposed to do, completely fall in his arms and let him take me on the conference table after someone called the office? Maybe whoever called pissed him off. Either way I should play it cool. The last thing I want is to seem desperate and clingy.

"Sure." I nod. "Let me help clean up and then we can go."

He doesn't look at me as he closes folder after folder, stacking them one on top of the other. "I'll stay behind and clean up. I've already called you a car. It's downstairs so you can go."

I'm stunned by his tone, but I'm not about to pry. Whoever he was just talking to has changed his mood completely, and I can't tell if it's for better or worse.

"Okay, well, I'll see you tomorrow then." I gather my things and nearly run out the door. He doesn't say anything else, and I'm grateful. For better or worse, I'm free of Johnathan for the night.

I STARE at the apartment door with disdain. The shadow of my brother dances under the door, oblivious to my early arrival. Once I open this door, I know it's going to be nothing but a streamline of questions. Maybe there's a bar around here that I can hide at until he passes out. He can't stay awake forever.

"I'm sure she'll be here in an hour or so." My brother's voice is muffled from the other side of the door. What, is he talking to Mom about the case too? Does everyone have to know my business these days?

"Oh, that's fine. I don't mind waiting."

That was definitely not Mom. I yank open the door to find a smart-looking man sitting on the couch. Jax sits on the loveseat across from him, his eyes landing on me the moment I walk inside.

"Hey, speaking of," Jax cheers, holding up a steaming mug. "Welcome home, little sister."

My eyes bounce from my brother to the stranger and back again. "What's going on?"

"Kylie, this is David Green. He's a good friend and colleague from the attorney general's office."

David nods to me. "It's a pleasure to meet you, Kylie. I've heard so much."

"All good things, I hope." I laugh nervously.

"A recent graduate and top candidate for the next generation of real estate agents." He smirks. "Your brother is very proud."

"Yeah, he's a blabbermouth." I lean on the wall and take off my shoes. This guy isn't here for me, and I'm grateful for the lack of interrogation. A few more polite words and I can play the tired card to escape.

"Let me ask you something, Kylie," David continues.

"Shoot." I grunt as I stow away my shoes on the top rack.

"What is a brilliant girl like you doing with a criminal like Johnathan Ronsberry?"

I freeze, my senses on high alert. Did Jax really tell a member of the attorney general's office about the case? How does he even know if he can trust this guy?

"And what would make you jump to such a wild conclusion?" I slowly rise and hike my bag higher on my shoulder. Let the interrogation begin.

"Have you ever heard the name Leonardo Guerra?" David sips from his own mug, the smell of chamomile lingering in the air.

"Can't say that I have," I lie and glare at my brother. "Jax, care to explain what the hell is going on here?"

"There's been talk around the office about Leo being involved in some shady practices." Jax stands. "We're not talking parking tickets or petty theft, Kylie. We're talking big. And based on your findings so far, we have a lot of reason to think that he's involved with the Ronsberrys beyond family matters."

"The Ronsberrys have a lot of business partners. That name hasn't crossed my desk once." I keep my tone neutral and feign a yawn. Better be careful not to give anything away.

"Maybe because they don't want you to find out," David says.

Jax makes his way toward me, as if I'm a lanternfly he's trying to put in a jar. "Kylie, we want you to help us catch Leonardo. We already know that he's connected to the Ronsberrys. We just need you to confirm how deep their ties go."

"Is this an official investigation?" I spit. "Why isn't the attorney general here at this late night meeting?"

"Well, let's just say when Leo Guerra is involved, there's always an investigation." David stands, buttoning his jacket. "He's the biggest mafia leader in New York. Our department has been watching him for a while."

Jax takes my hands, eyes pleading. "Kylie, if Johnathan has anything to do with Leonardo, you're not safe. If you are going to continue with this ridiculous hunt, at least help us put someone away in the process."

"I don't know what you are talking about." I snatch my hands away. "So much for being a good friend."

"Kylie—"

"Stop trying to pacify me like I'm a child!" I yell. "I've played along with your twenty questions because I know you're concerned. But this ambush that you've planned is crossing a line."

I snatch up my purse and shoes without a second thought and walk out the door.

"Kylie!" Jax yells, following me. "We're not done here."

"Oh, we're very much done here." I stomp toward the elevator. "You can keep talking with Sherlock Holmes over there, but I'm done."

The elevator door opens to let off a woman walking her dog, and I politely smile at her as she passes. Jax hangs on to my arm as I step inside and press the button for the lobby.

"Kylie, please," he begs, stepping onto the elevator with me. "You can't tell me you're not the least bit curious about how Leo is connected to all of this. You told me a few weeks ago that he was involved. Has something changed?"

"Back off, Jax!" I yell as I put on my shoes. "I'm not going to be your source anymore. I trust Johnathan. He doesn't bombard me with questions the moment I walk into the room. He trusts me."

"He's playing you." Jax groans, exasperated. "Look, I love Johnathan as much as the next guy, but his father is another story. He would've done anything to get into power, even if it meant making deals with the wrong people."

"So what do you want me to do? Spy on him?" I snap at him.

"All I'm asking is for you to get us proof. Something that we can use to bring Leonardo down once and for all. If you work with us, I can guarantee you full protection. Something Johnathan can't offer."

"Why, because you think he's some kind of mastermind criminal?"

"Because he's the CEO." Jax grabs my arm, forcing me to look at him. "Kylie, this isn't just me being overprotective. This is serious. I don't want you to get hurt."

The doors of the elevator open, and I take in his terrified expression. Worried or not, I don't care. I'm not about to go back upstairs and continue to be questioned.

"Goodnight, Jax." I step out into the lobby, and Jax's arm falls away in defeat. I'm sure whatever is going on doesn't involve Johnathan; he seems just as confused as I am. He confided in me, and I'm not about to abandon him now. His father may or may not have been a shady guy, but that doesn't mean his son is too. The sidewalk shines with fresh rain as I make my way back to Ronsberry Law Firm. If I'm going to find any real answers, it'll be in there.

CHAPTER 19

Johnathan

I FUCKING HATE ISABELLA.

I wave at a few of my men standing guard out front as I walk into the building. They insisted on being here early if I was going to be here, especially to meet with Isabella. I lean on the wall and wait for the elevator. How is it that I'm the one in charge and she's the one bossing me around? And what's gotten into her anyway? I've grown so used to her being in the background that I never expected her to start requesting private meetings out of nowhere. And now that my dad is gone…how convenient.

A surge of panic shoots through me. Is this the agreement my father was talking about? Is my marriage somehow roped into something worse than being chained to Isabella? My mind races all the way up to the fortieth floor. No wonder we've been hitting a wall these last few nights. I've been so focused on Kylie not finding about Isabella that I didn't even think to check her dad's files. If I'm going to figure this out, I need to fully trust her. Once I'm done talking with Isabella, I'll tell Kylie the truth. Hopefully she won't kill me, considering my latest discovery.

The office is quiet with no one in it. Different than the silent nights that I spend with Kylie. It's like the sunrise brings a quiet anticipation for the day. A serene kind of silence that I can use a bit more often. But today is not that kind of morning. The sunlight blinds me the moment I walk into my office. Jeez, did the cleaning crew forget to shut the blinds?

"Good morning!"

Her voice sets my heart into overdrive, and I shield my eyes to get a better look at the room. The conference table is once again littered with folders. Kylie sits in her usual chair, the same outfit she wore last night still on. Her hair has fallen loose around her shoulders, and I can't help but eye the few top buttons that have come undone. Even a bit disgruntled, she still looks like a dark beauty.

"Kylie," I say, voice strained. "What are you doing here? I thought I sent you home last night."

"Well, I came back." She shrugs, eyes glued to the papers. "I was planning on going home to change and grab some breakfast before you arrived, but here you are. Mr. Early Bird."

"You should go now then," I encourage. "Before everyone starts walking in, you can sneak out and get refreshed."

"I have a few pages left in this folder and then I'll go."

She's still lost in the thrill of the chase, oblivious to the panic stirring inside of me. I clear my throat and try to casually walk toward my desk. I have to figure out a way to get her out of here before—

"Knock, knock," Isabella's sing-song voice chimes as she throws the door open. Her eyes immediately fall on Kylie. "Oh, you already have your assistant working through the night. Very Frank Ronberry of you, Johnathan."

"Oh, she was just leaving," I stammer, sweat beading on my upper lip. "We can talk out in the hall while she—"

"Oh, I'm not concerned with the help. You know that." She waves her hand and walks into the room. "I won't be long, anyway. Like I said last night, I have a very busy day planned."

"Of course." I sigh, dropping my bag on my desk.

"We have some, let's just say...business to discuss," she states. "I thought we could discuss how we should proceed over dinner."

"Sure. Whatever you want," I say, trying not to show my hatred for her.

The sickly scent of her cotton candy perfume surrounds me as she closes in, those thin lips painted a streak of red as her hands play with my tie. The rustling of papers has stopped completely as Isabella inches closer. Every part of me wants to push her away. This isn't like Isabella. Normally she'd use physical contact as a last resort in her act as my wife, but here she is fixing my tie. Is it because of Kylie?

"I've already had my assistant make reservations at Le Chatue for eight. I expect you to handle the transportation."

"Naturally." I force the word out. I feel like I can't breathe, this is so uncomfortable.

She leans in and whispers in my ear. "Got to keep up appearances. It seems your little helper is interested in you. She's cute. But don't let it become a distraction."

She pulls away and waves with that plastic smile in place. "See you tonight."

I stare at Isabella in disbelief as she slinks out the room, the door slamming behind her. The peace of the morning is gone, and I'm left paralyzed behind my desk. Her words sent a shiver up my spine. Was it a threat or a warning? Even if she seemed part robot, that woman intuition seems to be just fine. But she's the least of my worries.

I can feel Kylie's eyes burning a hole into my left temple, but I don't dare move. What do I even say to her? Sorry for not telling you that I'm married, but I really didn't want you to find out this way? She's going to quit for sure. And just as I was putting the pieces together.

I finally find the courage to turn, and I'm surprised to find her staring at the last page of the folder instead of me. Her hands lay flat on the desk. I want to hold her in my arms and tell her everything, but she might stab me with a letter opener or something if I move too fast.

"Kylie," I croak, heart pounding. "Let me explain."

She slowly turns toward me, an eerie smile on her face. It's calm. A bit too calm for the given circumstance. I want to pour out the rest of the truth all at once but don't know where to start.

"You have a meeting in fifteen minutes," she says, voice neutral.

I blink at her. "What?"

"You have a meeting with Fawn Gregger in fifteen minutes on the twenty-seventh floor. Conference room A."

Her calm is jarring, almost robotic. Is she secretly planning to poison my lunch later as revenge?

"Kylie," I start, but she holds up a hand.

"The help is going home for a few hours." She rises to stand and stacks the folder she was reading on the top of the pile.

"I can call a car for you," I say, reaching for my phone.

"No need." She waves away the idea. "By the way, you should review your day before you leave. Looks like another busy one."

"Okay."

"I won't be back in the afternoon after you've had your lunch." Kylie looks me once over, a mix of emotions swirling behind her eyes.

I want to bring her in my arms, but I just watch helplessly as she grabs her bag and walks out the door without another word. I ease myself into the cushions of the office chair, eyes still glued to the door. At least she didn't quit on the spot. But she also isn't coming back anytime soon. This is a disaster. I lean on my desk, mind swirling faster than I can handle. What am I going to do now?

CHAPTER 20

Kylie

WHO THE FUCK WAS THAT? My blood boils as I wait to cross the street, the flashing stop sign mimicking how I feel inside. Maybe I've been wrong about him this entire time. Maybe he's been really good at playing me, and now he's just been busted.

The apartment building comes into view, and I numbly walk through the lobby. But I can't seem to shake this feeling. Something's not right; I can feel it in my gut. That kiss felt real, very real. I could almost feel his vulnerability, which is something he never shows. This is very problematic because it's adding to my confusion of wanting him last night and hating him right now.

However, one thing I've gotten really good at after my shit show of a marriage is reading people, and I owe it to myself to figure this out. I'm not stupid; I would have noticed something as close as we've been working. But I need to figure out what the fuck is going on.

My late night out gave me no more information than it did before. I can't help but wonder if there are other files hidden in the office. Files that Johnathan has kept hidden from me or I missed along with his mystery seductress.

A sea of kids bound off of the elevator, their backpacks bouncing behind them as they run through the lobby without a care in the world. Oh, what I wouldn't give to be one of them right now. I'd run so far no one would ever find me. An endless game of hide and seek.

Sleep calls for me as I stumble onto the elevator and watch the numbers climb. With any luck, Jax is already halfway to the office with his good friend David. I'm sure I'll get chewed out later once he gets home. Maybe I should switch things up and interrogate him for a change. Stay home and wait by the door in a robe and slippers like Mom. I pause on the threshold. Ah, sweet silence.

The apartment sits undisturbed as I walk inside, and I kick off my shoes. A hot shower and a nap should do the trick to relieve me of my fatigue. Maybe a shot of something after to ease the sting of what I just witnessed. Maybe two shots.

"Kylie?"

I jump a little as Jax pops his head out from behind the couch, his hair flat on one side. Was he waiting for me there all night?

"Hey, Jax." I nod his way before moving toward the hall. Whatever lecture he has planned can wait till later when I'm coherent.

"No, wait," he says, stumbling to a stand. "I want to apologize."

I shrug. "No need. You were right. I was wrong. End of story."

"I had no right to ambush you," he blurts out. "I told David to call the whole thing off once you left. It's not fair of me to ask those kinds of things of you. Especially if it will put you in danger."

"No kidding," I mumble, leaning on the wall to hold up my worn-out body. "Shouldn't you be at work?"

"Well, I can't just leave without knowing my sister came home safely. Besides, I think a day off will do me some good." He stretches with a yawn, and I can't help but yawn in response.

"You have been acting a little crazy lately," I admit.

"I promise from here on out not to interrogate you anymore," he vows, holding up a hand.

I'd appreciate this apology a little more if Johnathan didn't just prove him to be right. I want to tell Jax everything that happened, but I know it won't end well. The last thing I need is for him to storm into the office with his big-brother pants on.

"Thanks, Jax," I say through another yawn. "I think I'm going to go take a shower and a nap if that's cool with you."

I've never been so happy to stumble toward a bathroom in my life. Hopefully the sting of betrayal will wash away in the shower, and I'll be able to take a decent nap before returning to the office. And this time, I will find what I'm looking for.

IT'S after two by the time I return, and Johnathan is nowhere to be seen. Glad that he got the hint. His schedule reflects the rest of the day filled with back-to-back meetings, so I don't anticipate him waltzing through the door anytime soon. Hopefully I can dig up what he's been hiding before the end of the day. I don't think I can take any more half-assed truths from him, and I'm definitely not going to sit around waiting for an explanation. It's time that I took matters into my own hands. And it starts with Leonardo Guerra.

I pile the folders we've searched through on the window ledge to make some room for four large boxes of files that have been collecting dust in the corner. When I first showed them to Johnathan, he reassured me that he knew exactly what this was and that it had nothing to do with our investigation. But with his new character revealed, I'm convinced that this is exactly what we've been looking for. And all I have to do is crack open the first box to be proven right.

Endless correspondence with Frank and Leo

about properties, some of while I've already read the files on. Agreements for wire transfers of large amounts to offshore bank accounts. It's like half of the dead ends I've been scratching my head over are in this one box alone. Did Johnathan know this was here all along? And if he did, does that mean our late-night meetings have been nothing but a ploy to get under my skirt? Was that really the challenge?

CHAPTER 21

Johnathan

S HE'S HERE.

I make my way toward her, heart pounding. How much has she been able to uncover in the last couple of hours? While I was busy in meetings, all I could do was imagine what Kylie was thinking. How betrayed she must feel after seeing me with Isabella. I'm grateful that she actually came back. If I was her, I'd have left out the front door and never returned. Maybe our time together goes a little deeper than I've been catering to.

She moves a box out of my way as I sit across from her. I lace my fingers on the table in front of me and take a deep breath. Time to come clean.

"I know there's a lot I have to apologize for," I start.

"Did you know about Leonardo?" she asks.

"Um, what about him exactly?" I stammer,

completely thrown off. "The fact that he's my father-in-law or—"

"What? Are you fucking kidding me? You're married?" she yells. I can see the shock on her face, and I quickly realize she didn't know Isabella is my wife.

Way to dig myself into a deeper hole.

"Look, Kylie."

"Don't Kylie me," she snaps. "Admit it. You've been playing me this whole time. This so-called mission you're after has nothing to do with the firm. Does it?"

I wipe away the sweat on my upper lip. "How much do you know?"

"A lot." She slides a folder across the table.

I flip through it with a growing rage. Every page unfolds a laundry list of lies my father has been feeding me. "My dad and Leo have been doing all of this behind my back?"

"Oh, don't pretend that you didn't know," she snaps.

I don't have enough fucks to give about Kylie's tone as I stand up and slam the folder on the desk. "Where the fuck did you find this?" I ask, fuming in a rage only Isabella can bring out in me.

"What are you talking about? They were in that box of folders by the window." She aggressively plants herself in a chair, waiting for my reaction while glaring at me like she's caught me red handed in a lie.

Of course. Those were the boxes that Isabella had sent over while she was moving offices after my dad died. She said they were real estate dealings for her office, and personal paperwork including our agreement aka nightmare of a marriage. Now the rage made sense. She was keeping these files hidden in plain sight, knowing I'd probably be secretly trying to find this information everywhere else and not think to question her if she was forthcoming. I swear that woman is the devil.

I rifled through page after page. "How could he do this to me? I did everything for him. Followed whatever task he asked of me without question. Everything! Down to the marriage license and it still wasn't enough?"

I kick over a chair in frustration, letting out a scream.

Kylie slowly rises from her seat, hands raised in surrender. "Okay, so maybe you didn't know about the money laundering."

"Ya think?" I fume, shooting daggers at her. "Kylie, my dad roped me into a scam. He had me marry Isabella for the betterment of his wallet, not the company that I helped keep alive for the last seven years. I bet the rest of these boxes hold the rest of his schemes and secrets. Fuck!"

I throw a chair across the room in a fury, an uncontrollable rage coming over me. Everywhere I look, I still see glimpses of him. I'm both haunted and cursed. And it's all because of him.

I stomp over to the line of photos on the wall and yank one off its hook, smashing it to pieces.

"Johnathan!" Kylie yells, but I ignore her.

One by one I slam the photos of my father's smug face onto the ground. I bet he's laughing up at me from hell right now. The bastard.

I slam the final photo on the ground with satisfaction.

Kylie stands quietly by the conference table, head tilted to the side. "Are you done?"

"Yes." I sigh, the fight leaving me. I adjust my jacket and walk back over to her, the shattered glass clinking under my feet. "Sorry. I didn't mean to show you that side of me."

"I've been seeing a lot of sides of you today." She smirks.

"I don't love Isabella. I never have. It was all arranged by our fathers," I blurt out.

Kylie blinks at me, completely stunned. I'm not sure why I said it, but it feels good finally saying it out loud.

"I don't expect you to believe me or trust anything I say ever again. But if you had to believe anything about me, believe that."

She stares at me, eyes searching mine. For what I'm not sure. She looks away with a heavy sigh and sits back in her chair. "I don't know what to believe anymore."

"Believe what you think is right." I shrug.

"I don't know the answer to that either." She

chuckles sadly.

"Neither do I."

I pick up the chair I kicked over and set it back at the table. Even in my fit of rage, the only thing that didn't survive were those photos. It's cathartic in a sense. Out with the old and in with the new. Although now thinking about it, I could've just thrown them in the trash.

CHAPTER 22

Kylie

"I REALLY DON'T KNOW what I've gotten myself into," I say to break the long silence.

"Ya, you and me both…" Johnathan aggressively rubs his hands over his temples.

I can clearly see the anguish on his face, and I know something isn't quite right. If he was "in the know" about this whole thing, he was really good at keeping up this whole "not knowing" facade. But to my surprise, I can see through the anguish, and I feel my heart go out to him, like I can sense the pain in his soul. For some weird reason, I still trust him, but I don't know why, so I'm going to table that for now. I don't know if it was because of the other night, but I want to help him figure this out. Then I can leave and find another job.

"Well, I can't say that I completely trust you, but I'd like to help."

"That's fair," he says, looking up, gazing past me

as he's consumed by his own thoughts. "And I'd appreciate the help." His phone buzzes and he takes it out to see the notification. "I gotta go." He sighs, sliding his phone back into his pocket.

"I'll keep this up for a few more hours and then go home," I say flippantly, trying to act like I've shut down all romantic feelings for him. "Enjoy your dinner tonight," I uncontrollably blurt out, hoping to punch him in the stomach with those words. Guess it's going to take more work to get rid of those feelings completely.

"Thanks," he grumbles as he walks out.

CHAPTER 23

Johnathan

IN THE CHAOS of the day, I completely forgot about my little meeting with my viper of a wife. I make my way back out the door. Maybe this conversation tonight will be a good thing. Maybe I'll finally be able to set myself free.

I STAND OUTSIDE of Le Chatue, tapping my foot impatiently. I sent for Isabella's car over an hour ago and she still hasn't shown up. So much for our reservations. I hope Kylie got home safe. When I called back at the office to check in before arriving at the restaurant, she was gone. I doubt that she would've thought to call downstairs and ask for someone to take her home. We have so many cars at our disposal, it's almost excessive. Especially when most of our meetings need no more than an elevator ride. Speaking of business…

The black company-issued car rolls around the corner, and I take a deep breath, a cloud of smoke forming as I exhale. If I'm going to get out of this deal, I have to play it cool. Time to put my skills as a lawyer to the test.

I hold open the door for Isabella and extend my hand out to her. "I hope they'll still seat us. It's long past our reservation."

"No, it's not." She grabs my hand for support and walks past me.

"You texted six o'clock."

"Yes, for my car to be ready," she snaps, flinging open the door to the restaurant.

I'm surprised the glass doesn't shatter with the force I slam the car door. This might be impossible to get through if all I want to do is wring her scrawny neck. I follow her inside to my doom. Let the games begin.

The hostess recognizes Isabella at a glance and quickly scrambles for two menus before leading us away. Her heels clack loudly with every step, and a few people stare at us as we pass. The kind of looks reserved for royalty or celebrities. I faintly catch the whispers about us from a nearby table. The king and queen of the Ronsberry firm are out for a stroll. Great. My reputation is now something people discuss over soup and oyster crackers. The sooner I can talk to Isabella about our deal, the better.

Our table sits separate from the rest. A hand-painted portrait of a woman and man dancing hangs above us, and I unbutton my jacket before having a seat.

Isabella looks down at her menu with pursed lips. Even doing something as simple as ordering a meal makes her look so unsatisfied. I guess Saint Isabella isn't making an appearance today. Although, judging by the reaction of the hostess, appearances aren't necessary here.

"So," I pick up my own menu, "what's good here?"

"Everything here sucks except the liquor." She scoffs.

"Weren't you the one that chose this place?"

"Indeed."

She sets down her menu and laces her fingers in front of her. It seems like we're not here to eat after all.

"What do you want to discuss?" I ask, glancing up from my menu. "Specifically, I mean."

"As you know, our agreement was both signed by our fathers. But with Frank out of the picture, that contract is now null and void."

I do my best not to jump out of my chair and scream with excitement. I can hardly contain my smile. How did I not think of this?

"So I want fifty percent of your company," she says smugly, clearly enjoying the fade of my excitement.

I snap my focus from the entrees to her stupidly pinched face. "Excuse me?"

"See, we are still legally married, and since we had the contract in place, there was no need for a prenup. Not to mention you didn't have squat to your name, so it was an easy oversight on your part."

Oh my God…this is not happening…

"Face it, Johnathan. You're in way over your head here."

She actually smiles at me. Smiles at me! The restraint it's taking for me not to leap across the table and strangle her right now is almost unbearable.

A waiter stops at our table and places a basket of bread rolls between us. "Your usual, Mrs. Ronsberry?"

"Make it a double, James." Isabella sighs, leaning back in her chair with a smirk. "My husband and us have a lot to discuss tonight."

"Of course." He bows before leaving, not bothering to take my order.

I'm numb, my thoughts racing back to when we signed the agreement. She's right, our fathers signed the agreement; there was no need for a prenup. My father made sure nothing was in my name for this very reason, hers as well. It seemed like a normal business transaction. The agreement wasn't long, and our fathers weren't that old and in decent health. How in the fuck did this happen?

"No fucking way! Never gonna happen!" I yell louder than expected.

"Calm down, Johnathan. The way I see it here, you don't have much of a choice," Isabella says as if I never spoke at all. "We are married, and you acquired the business within our marriage. Not much to dispute." My objections do not faze her at all.

I'm floored. I can't even begin to wrap my head around what she's saying.

"But just to make this easier, I'm willing to compromise."

There's more? She goes on. "You sign over fifty percent of the company, and you won't have to explain to that little mouse you have in your office why your wife is pregnant."

I think I'm going to pass out as the blood rushes to my head. "I haven't touched you since we've been married!" I'm getting tunnel vision now; I can't hear any people or see anyone but her and the smile that's appearing across her face. This time it's different; she knows she's won. I've seen that smile before when she's secured her biggest real estate deals for pennies on the dollar.

"But there was a time you did…Johnathan…" She leans forward, touching my hand and tracing her finger around my knuckles.

I think back to how she helped secure the deal in the first place. I had grown closer to Isabella as the two families had begun their business courtship. I was told they were real estate developers, which they also were. And our two real estate development companies would join hands. Our building and purchasing power would become unmatched. Isabella and my presence was requested during several meetings as we were the heirs and the bond to this business relationship. But we'd escape off to the side and let our fathers talk business. She knew what was being asked of her. She didn't seem to mind, so we had a few fun nights of our own.

The waiter returns with two glasses, placing Isabella's standard cosmopolitan drink in front of her and a glass of dark-colored liquid in front of me. One whiff lets me know it's a rum and Coke. My favorite. I can't help but wonder if it's poisoned. I wouldn't put it past her.

"We always used condoms." I was starting to feel the defeat at this point. I could almost already anticipate her answer.

"Exactly, which worked out wonderfully. We have embryos!"

She's insane. She was definitely part of the bigger plan. I'm sick.

"Daddy will be so happy that we've sorted everything out." She smiles, taking a sip of her drink with a little bounce in her seat "He will have a new contract drawn up for you to sign at Frank's celebration of life party tomorrow night. Kind of fitting, don't you think? End of an old era, and beginning of a new...let's just say smarter and younger generation." The first time I see her happy and it's at the loss of my freedom.

I take the chance and gulp my own dark drink, fear bubbling up faster than I can quell it. This wasn't a meeting at all. Isabella planned this down to the rum and Coke.

When I get to the office tomorrow, I need to find something to pin on Leo. I've been tricked by the devil's spawn herself.

CHAPTER 24

Kylie

"She's nuts. Completely psycho!"

I sit at my usual spot as Johnathan paces back and forth, a morning bagel gripped in my left hand. He has been going on nonstop since I walked through the door. I've never seen him so distraught, and the more he talks, the more I'm concerned. Not only is Johnathan at risk of being trapped in a life he hates, but his company is getting swiped right out from under him by his own wife. I break off another piece of my bagel and pop it into my mouth.

"I'm sure we can find something on Leo. We just have to keep looking."

"And then what?" he yells, exasperated. "If I go to the police, they'll just take me to jail right along with Leo. Ronsberry Law Firm will be history."

I think about my deal with Jax and can't help but feel guilty. I called him after I found out about Isabella and told him I'd help gather some information on Leo. I was having mixed emotions at the time and convinced myself it was the only way to possibly help Johnathan out of a dangerous situation when I clearly knew it was also out of spite. Now here I am munching on breakfast while Johnathan's whole life falls apart.

"We will figure something out," I say gently. "But we have to keep our heads if we're going to figure this out."

Johnathan sighs with frustration, the muscles in his jaw tight with anger and worry. How is he supposed to go through the day like this? One more piece of bad news and he might lose it completely.

"Have you found anything else?" He looks at me, eyes pleading for good news.

"I'm still piecing everything together, but there's good reason to think that Leo owns more property than he lets on." With his reputation being as bad as Jax says, I'm not surprised.

Johnathan collapses into a nearby chair and hides his face in his hands. I want to reach out and comfort him, but I don't move. That ship sailed with the revelation of the truth.

"Maybe you should take the day off," I suggest. "A day to clear your mind and do whatever rich people do to get right again."

"I can't," he groans. "If I do, Isa will probably get suspicious and tighten my leash. Not to mention, I have to find something soon. Or that's it, I'm losing fifty percent of the company. But I have a feeling that's just the tip of the iceberg. She's never going to leave my life."

He rises to a stand and shoots me a tired smile. "You have no idea how much I appreciate what you are doing."

I shoot him a thumbs-up as the guilt sinks deeper at his words. If he only knew. "I've got your back."

Johnathan nods before leaving the office, and I scramble for my phone the moment the door slams closed. I need to talk to Jax. If Johnathan is in this much trouble, there has to be something that he can do to help.

"Hello, Jax speaking."

"Hey, we need to talk about the plan."

"Hold on." The sound of rustling can be heard on the other end. "Okay. Sorry. I don't need anyone eavesdropping while we talk. People are here can be super nosey."

"You must fit right in then," I muse.

"Hilarious. So, what did you find? Or did you just call to harass me?"

"Johnathan just had a complete meltdown over the dinner with his wife," I explain. "She's threatening to take half of his company. But he thinks she's not going to stop there."

"What!" Jax yells. "That will give Leo a direct line to all of the firm's important files."

"And would leave little room to keep Johnathan around."

"Do you think that he killed Frank?" Jax asks.

"I don't know, but I'll be staying here late to figure it out. We're running out of time to nail this."

"Don't worry. David and I will figure out how to get Leo one way or another. If this gets too dangerous, I'm getting you out of there. No discussion."

"I know." I sigh. "I was wondering if David could get some kind of deal for Johnathan too."

"Kylie, he's married into a family of criminals. There's nothing I can do."

"But he had no idea this was happening," I protest. "He's scared, Jax. Can you just try to see if you can do something?"

Jax sighs on the other end. "I'll try."

"Thanks."

The line goes dead, and I savor the last bite of my bagel. The other two large boxes sit untouched at the opposite end of the table. Reality is setting in... I'm scared too. I can deny it all I want, but I've formed a connection with Johnathan. And he could be going away for a long time if I can't help him. The thought makes my heart hurt. The more we investigate, the more my spite disappears, and anger seems to be taking its place. Not at Johnathan this time, but at Isabella. Even if she sees me as nothing more than the help, I'm starting to see what that woman is capable of. I'd never admit it to Johnathan, but have a feeling I should not be angry; I should be very afraid.

CHAPTER 25

Johnathan

ANOTHER LONG-ASS DAY. I highly doubt that Kylie stayed behind this late to do research, but I'm itching to dig in those folders and see what she's uncovered. The familiar light of the lamp still glows as I walk into my office. She's a dark beauty amongst the shadows, hair falling around her shoulders as she thumbs through another folder.

"You stayed," I say, surprised.

"I figured you'd want to dig through these after your day was over. I didn't want you messing up my system."

Her tone is light, the anger from yesterday gone completely. It's almost like the last twenty-four hours didn't happen and it's another late night. Just the two of us.

"So should I wait to call the Chinese restaurant or just place the order now?"

"Absolutely not. You still owe me pizza!"

I hold up my hands in surrender. "It's just pizza, Kylie."

"Maybe to you." She sighs. "But I've been so busy helping you out that I've been slacking on my touristy to-do list. A girl has priorities, you know."

"You've never had New York pizza?" I gasp.

"Is that a bad thing?" Kylie asks with a playful smirk.

I fully walk into the room and toss my bag onto my desk. It's not long before I'm grabbing her hand and yanking her out of her manilla folder.

"Get up. We're leaving."

"What? Where are we going?" she stammers.

I look down with a smirk. "To the best pizza spot in town."

"ARE you sure it's okay for us to be out like this?" Kylie shuffles beside me on the sidewalk as we make our way towards Sal's.

"If the viper queen wants to make an appearance, let her." I shrug. "I'm taking my assistant out for pizza. Nothing too glamorous in my opinion."

"True."

She is so cute when she's nervous, the small fidget of her hands along the hem of her sweater giving her away. Her shoulder brushes against my arm, and a zap of electricity flows through me. This is the first time that we're going out since dinner with Jax and this time we're all alone. Does this count as a date? I know that I just told Kylie not to worry, but as she continues to electrocute me with her touch, I can't help but wonder.

"Here we are," I sing, presenting the busted storefront.

Kylie's eyebrow raises with concern. "Are you sure this is the place?"

"What, did you think everything in New York was like Fifth Avenue?" I laugh, holding the cracked door open for her.

The smell of pizza wafts onto the sidewalk, and Kylie doesn't hesitate to walk inside. Score one for Johnathan. The place is only big enough for a handful of tables and chairs. Two giant brick ovens that sit side by side take up the rest of the real estate. Kylie looks around like a kid at Disneyland. Is this really her first time in a pizza shop?

"Johnnyboy!"

I turn to see Sal walking toward me, his apron covered in flour. "Hey. What are you still doing here this late?"

"I can't let these new kids handle everything." Sal laughs. "Got to do things to keep the old mind right."

"I hear that."

Sal's smile falls a little. "I'm sorry to hear of your father's passing. He was a good man."

Sure he was. I politely nod and point at the slices in the window. "Give me two cheese slices to sooth my sorrows."

"You got it." Sal's eyes trail over Kylie. "And for your girlfriend?"

"Oh, no. I'm not his girlfriend," Kylie stammers. "I'm his assistant."

Sal blushes a little. "My mistake."

"This is her first time eating New York pizza, so give her something good." I smile.

Sal's eyes go wide, his blush gone. "A foreigner! Well, why didn't you say so?"

He turns and disappears back into the kitchen, a few inaudible commands yelled in the distance. Leave it to the old man to want to impress Kylie on my account. I walk toward one of the metal chairs and take a seat. Kylie follows my lead and sits beside me, head on a swivel as she continues to admire the place.

"So, care to share what you've found out so far?" I ask.

She stops sightseeing long enough to glare at me. "You and Jax are exactly the same, you know that?"

"We get that a lot." I chuckle. "There was a rumor going around campus that we were fraternal twins separated at birth. I started it, naturally."

"I'd believe it." She glances around one last time before resting those dark eyes on me. "Can we not talk about the case while we eat?"

"Well, then what do you want to talk about?"

"How about the reason why a rich boy such as yourself knows about a place like this?"

She smirks at me as I take in the stained white

walls under florescent lights with a smile. "My dad used to take me here when I was a kid. Used to boast that one day he'd buy the place and retire selling pizza. I thought he was nuts. But that was before he changed into someone I hardly knew."

"Do you miss him?"

I take in the care in her eyes and feel a twinge of pain in my chest. "It's hard to miss someone who has screwed you over in more ways than one. But yeah. I guess. I guess I haven't thought about it too much."

"Asshat or not, he was still your dad. You must've had some good memories of him."

"All the good memories I have are probably left in this very spot." I smile at her. "I'm glad that I'm able to keep up the tradition."

Her cheeks flush, and she looks away, a wide grin on her face. Sal comes out with an extra-large box and a white paper bag.

"All right," he grunts as he puts it on the table next to me. "Half cheese, half pepperoni, with garlic knots on the side. My treat."

"Aw, Sal. You didn't have to." I stand and clap him on the back.

"Your father was a loyal customer and a good friend," Sal says with tears in his eyes. "And I know that wherever he is, he's super proud of you, Johnathan."

I think about the boxes of evidence that say otherwise and manage to force a small smile. "Thanks, Sal."

He turns toward Kylie and points a thumb my way. "Take good care of this guy right here."

"Yes, sir," Kylie says with pride. Sal nods at us with approval and walks back to the kitchen with nothing more than a wave of his hand.

I look over at Kylie and grab onto the pizza box. "Ready to go?"

"We're not eating it here?" she asks, voice small with disappointment.

Even when she isn't trying to, she can be the most adorable person I've ever met. I sit back in my seat and flip open the box. "I give you first dibs."

My mouth waters as she pulls a slice from the pie, the cheese hanging off the side in one long string. I secure my own slice and capture the stray cheese with my tongue. Kylie's face lights up as she takes her first bite, the slice looking huge in her tiny mouth. Kind of like how I had her back on the island. I swallow my own first bite of pizza and try to think of anything else. But the more she eats, the more I can't stop thinking about it. My pants get tighter by the second, and I'm grateful she's sitting across from me this time.

"I see why people rave about this stuff." Kylie licks her lips.

A bit of sauce sits on the corner of her mouth, and I can't help but imagine myself licking it off. Oh, this is impossible. I calmly stand up and walk over to the napkin stand on the counter, grateful that Sal is busy in the kitchen instead of out here. Nice as he is, he's not the kind of guy that passes up an opportunity to make a quick joke at another's expense. The last thing I want Kylie to think is that I only hired her for sex. Not that I would mind putting my face in between those thighs again.

I grab a handful of napkins and try to casually hold them in front of my growing desires. Kylie's too invested in the pizza to notice. I park myself back behind the safety of the pizza box and hold out some napkins to her.

"Don't forget about those garlic knots. They are to die for."

"Okay."

She goes for the kill and rips the bag wide open, stuffing a garlic knot in her mouth.

"Mmm," she moans as she chews. "This is so good."

"I'm glad you like it," I say, voice slightly strained as he continues to moan.

I have to get it together. If I make one wrong step, my future is over. The signing is in a few days, and Kylie is my last hope in stopping it. No way am I about to piss her off over something as trivial as lust. Even if my desires make me want to burst at the sight of her stuffing her mouth, I can't do anything but watch. Not until I'm completely free.

CHAPTER 26

Kylie

THAT WAS the best pizza I've ever had. I walk slowly next to Johnathan as we cross the street, overstuffed on cheese and bread.

"I can't believe I've been missing out this whole time." I nudge him. "And you just kept letting me order chicken lo mien?"

"In my defense, Jax should've taken you there the moment you got here." He laughs.

"You both are hopeless."

As soon as I say it, my foot catches on the sidewalk, tumbling me forward to my doom. Johnathan's arms are around me before I hit the ground, and I lean into him to regain my balance.

"Thanks," I say, breathless.

The scent of the pizzeria still lingers on his jacket. My heartbeat is all I can hear as I look at him, his hands still holding onto the small of my back.

"Completely hopeless," he breathes, moving a stray strand of hair out of my eyes.

I need to move away from him. Now. The chances of Isabella showing up were unknown, and I don't need Johnathan losing everything because of my clumsiness.

"We should get back to the office," I whisper, the air cold enough to see our breath.

I want him to ignore my words and kiss me on this street corner. Even though he kept secrets from me, I don't care. It's not like I'm not keeping things from him now. But his warmth fades with his heavy sigh and he shoves his hands in his coat pocket. "Yeah. Let's get back."

He doesn't look at me as we walk silently down the street, and I'm grateful. One look and he'll probably see though me and all my desires. And I'm losing the strength to say no.

CHAPTER 27

Johnathan

I YAWN from the backseat as I'm driven to my dad's place. It's been a while since I've been there, and I was lowkey hoping I'd never have to come back. But with my mother constantly nagging me to come over, I figured I might as well get it out of the way. With Kylie working hard in the office, it might do me some good to get away from the endless drone of meetings. One more conversation about the future of the company and I might go insane.

The car pulls into the roundabout of my dad's estate, and I brace myself for the awaited scolding of my mother. She stands at the top of the steps, her foot tapping with impatience. I haven't even gotten out of the car yet and she's already pissed. Better make this a quick visit.

"Hey, Mom." I wave, slamming the car door closed.

"You're late."

She walks inside without waiting for me, and I climb the stairs two at a time to catch up with her.

"Honestly, Johnathan. I don't know why you haven't bothered to come here sooner. You will have to maintain this property sooner or later."

"One fire at a time, please," I snap. "I'm trying to keep the entire company afloat."

"Which is even more reason for you to have come here sooner." She leads me down the marble staircase to my dad's study, the familiar musk surrounding us as I step inside. Compared to his office at the firm, this place is lavish. A clean desk and sofa in pristine condition. Not even a single document sticks out from the bookshelves lining the walls. I guess he doesn't have much to hide in his own home. My mom walks over to a massive painting of my dad and stands in front of it, admiring him with a sigh.

"Here's the safe your dad was talking about."

I watch as she pulls back the massive frame like a door. The lock of a safe stares back at me, and my mother motions for me to come closer. I guess I spoke too soon.

"What is this?"

"What do you mean what is this? Isn't that why you came over?" My mom looked as confused as I was. "This is the safe your dad wanted you to get into if anything ever happened to him. In the hospital, he said he was going to tell you about it and for me to show you the door."

Clearly that's one of the things my dad didn't get around to telling me... "What do you mean? Where did this come from? What's in there?" I ask, trying to piece all of my thoughts together from the hospital, and his last words to me, none of which ever mentioned a safe.

"He never told you about this? I was wondering why it was taking you so long to come over. He had it installed seven years ago. And he was very clear about stressing the importance of you getting your hands on whatever it is that he left you inside if anything ever happened to him."

"Seven years ago? How did I not know about this?" I regretted that question the minute I heard it out loud.

"Really? I have hardly seen you in this house besides on holidays for the last ten years. Maybe if you'd come over more oft—"

"What's the code?" I cut her off as to not have this turn into another lecture. My heart was now racing, I was already feeling sick wondering what other mess he'd left behind. I don't know how I went from lawyer to investigator in such a short time span, but I'm not cut out for this.

"I have no idea. He said you would know." I hear my mother's footstep recede back up the staircase. *Way to be cryptic, Dad.* I stare at the shiny metal of the safe for a while as it seems to stare back at me.

Seven years ago...what could be so important seven years ago? I think as I rack my brain for a number combination that might work. Then it hits me. I punch in some numbers on the automated keypad as it comes to life. My phony wedding date. A shot in the dark but if I know the old man he's not that complicated when it comes to numbers. I hear the lock click, I turn the knob, and it opens with ease, and I laugh bitterly. Of course he would tie it back to that forsaken agreement.

The door creaks back, and I step inside, a few lights springing to life. The safe was small. Probably the size of a closet with some shelves lining the inside.

But there are few boxes that immediately catch my eye. I crack one open and quickly sift through it. Just scanning the first few pages confirms that I've hit the jackpot. Signed agreements between Leo and my father along with what looks like some recordings, and there are a couple of jump drives labeled by date and year. Everything looks eerily organized especially compared to the mess he left in his office. He clearly wanted me to be able to find something in here. I tear open another box to see a handwritten letter with my name on the front.

Words from beyond the grave. I unfold the paper to skim it over and blanch at the words.

"If you're reading this, Leo must've finally made his move."

He talks as if Leo was out to get him from the very beginning. Everything from videos to correspondence sits in this one box, and I can feel the hope bubbling up inside of me. Each one of these boxes holds more of the missing clues I've been searching for. This is probably something Isabella would kill to get her hands on. No wonder the old man took the time to build this safe. The last person that needs to know about any of this is her.

I'm about to close the last box back up when I notice the glint of metal catch my eye. I push back a few files and pull out the rusted keychain from Sal's. An envelope of cash hangs off the end, the words "buy Sal's" scribbled on the front. I chuckle to myself and stick it back at the bottom of the box. Even in the end, he was still serious about buying that pizzeria. Don't worry, Dad. I won't forget your dreams. But first I have to secure mine. And it starts by getting these boxes back to the office. Now.

CHAPTER 28

Kylie

"What the fuck is all that?"

I watch from my desk as Johnathan drops a large box down on the conference table, followed by a couple of other men with boxes who follow suit.

"Thank you, gentleman. That will be all," Johnathan says, ushering them out the room.

Johnathan waits until the door slams closed to look at me, a new fire in his eyes. "You're never going to believe what I just found."

The nights fly by as Johnathan and I continue to piece together a solid case for his freedom. I used to be so angry at Isabella for barging into the office that day, but now I'm grateful. Because of her, we're able to create a solid case to get Johnathan out of this forceful agreement once and for all. And with Jax working tirelessly behind the scenes, we'll get to put her and Leo away on the side.

Those boxes ended up having more pieces that we were looking for. All the information we've been sorting through for the last few weeks have been like trying to put together a giant, fucked-up puzzle with missing pieces. Thank god Johnathan might have found some of the missing pieces.

An entire box of back-up documents sits on the window ledge as I try my best to piece together their arrangement. It became apparent very quickly that Frank clearly did not trust Leo and seemed to be hedging his bets, because he made copies of everything. I can only assume he did this in case things went awry. Hidden copies in a hidden safe definitely paints a picture of someone who's concerned they might be the one who gets screwed over.

I'll give it to Frank, looking through all of this paperwork, you could tell he was a good businessman. But Johnathan said the money didn't drive him anymore; he had enough money. It was power. Power was what gave him a rush that he soon became addicted to. This is when he started finessing the most powerful political relationships he could. And he had accumulated quite the political circle of favors, when one night he saw the opportunity to seize more power. He had met Leo at an event, and although he understood exactly what that family stood for, he didn't hesitate at the opportunity to connect himself to him. Leo was a powerhouse in real estate as well, and that was pretty much all Johnathan knew.

Judging by a recording he had saved from their first meeting, Leo had made a proposal that Frank couldn't refuse. They planned to join forces to launder money, buy property, and utilize his political relationships to make sure that their businesses could grow with no interference. It seemed simple enough on the surface. But with this arrangement came power, and both sides wanted reassurance. Frank saw this as a foolproof way for both of them to have equal stake in the game. Nothing could be simpler than an arranged marriage. But he was wrong.

What Frank didn't know at the time was that Leonardo Guerra was not a man of fairness. He wanted it all, including Frank's political power. And for the last seven years, Johnathan said Leo worked on developing plenty of those political ties through Frank. The more years that pass led to more fake companies, nonexistent properties, and real estate deals.

But Johnathan seems to be focused on finding something that can help him with what's haunting him the most: Johnathan and Isabella's marriage.

"Do you think Leo killed your dad?" I whisper to Johnathan one night.

"I don't know." He shrugs. "But I wouldn't put it past him after reading all of this."

If there is one thing that we are both sure of, it is that even if this case is dangerous, we aren't giving up without a fight.

Massive amounts of correspondence—emails, recordings, and paperwork—built a solid case against Leo and his associates almost overnight. I take the time to scan everything onto a jump drive while Johnathan is in meetings throughout the day so I can show Jax and his own team can continue to build his own case against Leo. There is no way I am going to be able to sneak all those files out of here without someone raising some serious questions. And even though I've been surviving on pizza and coffee for the last forty-eight hours, and all my senses tell me to be more afraid for my own life at this point, I feel more alive than ever.

Johnathan hovers over the folder with the final plan as I stifle a yawn, his brow creased in concern as he flips the page.

I groan and walk away from the table. "We've been over this a hundred times. There's enough here. I'm sure of it."

"I don't know," he grumbles. "I can't help but feel like we're missing something."

There's doubt in his voice, and I can't seem to find the right words to make it go away. I take the risk of walking back to the table and gently putting my hand on his, the sparks between us tingling the palm of my hand.

"You've got this," I say. "If anyone can pull this off, it's you."

"Thanks." He turns to me with a small smile. "I could have never gotten this far without you."

"Oh, what are personal assistants for?" I laugh nervously, removing my hand from his.

"Seriously, Kylie. I don't know what I would do without you."

His eyes search mine as if begging me to understand. But whatever he wants me to know is still a mystery to me. The fatigue I felt is but a memory as I get lost in his gaze. He's like a magnet that I can't resist. And this time, I don't. I lean into him, gently pressing my lips to his, and quickly pull away. Just a little peck to calm my frail nerves. Completely harmless. But Johnathan has other plans. One look and I can tell that I've awakened the beast.

His hands are on the small of my back as he leads me back toward him.

"Where do you think you're going?" he whispers, biting his lip.

"Um." I have no words. He looks down at my lips and meets my gaze as he leans in closer. I know that I should push him away. Break the tension with a lame joke that ruins the mood so we can go home and focus on the mission at hand. But the longer I stare at him, the more I can't pull away. What's one more kiss between us going to hurt?

I lean into him, lips back on mine as he kisses me over and over. His hands trail down to my ass and grip it tight. I can feel his desires pressing against me, and it stirs my insides. I can't help but bite his lip a little, and a low growl escapes him. His hands slide under my skirt, and I stifle a moan as he slides past my panties.

"Already soaked, I see," he breathes. "Just like last time."

"It's hard not to feel this way around you," I admit, my cheeks hot with desire. He slides his fingers inside me without hesitation, and I relish in his touch. My hands grip the edge of the conference table as he continues to please me.

"Did you miss my touch?" he asks, rubbing his thumb on my clit.

"Yes," I moan, unable to hold it in any longer.

He slips out of me long enough to flip me around and press my torso down onto the table. The sound of his belt coming undone makes me squirm in anticipation. The scent of him fills the air and my mouth waters. I long to run my tongue up and down his shaft like last time, but I don't dare move. Not that I wouldn't mind a little punishment from him.

"You won't be needing these anymore." He laughs darkly, sliding my panties to the ground.

My eyes cross as the length of him slides inside of me. Oh, how I've missed this. He grips my ass and thrusts father. Deeper.

"Fuck," I moan, losing whatever little restraint I had left.

He moves faster. "You like that?"

"Yes," I breathe, doing my best not to be too loud. Even if we are normally the last ones here, I don't want to take any chances.

I feel him retreat but not for long. He spins me back to face him and kisses me deeply.

"Hang on," he whispers, lifting me off the ground.

I wrap my legs around him, and his dick slides right inside me. It's so big, I feel like I'm going to split in two the deeper he goes. He manages to press my back against the wall, and I run my fingers through his hair as I cum over and over again.

"Johnathan," I yell, unable to hold back.

I squeeze my thighs around his waist as he moves faster. This is better than the island. Before, I was pleasing a stranger in the dark, unsure what the morning would bring and not caring either way. Now, everything feels different. The last few weeks we've spent together have given us as chance to learn each other in so many ways. The look in his eyes isn't clouded over like back then. This is more than just lust-filled passion. Is it possible that this is love?

"Kylie," he breathes.

The way he says my name makes me gush on the spot. If everything goes well tomorrow, Johnathan will be a free man by the end of the day. And maybe there will be a slim chance for us to try things beyond the late-night study sessions.

Deep down, I know that this moment won't last. Sooner or later this ecstasy will end, and we'll be back to our normal lives. I don't think I can continue pretending that this feeling doesn't exist. And no matter how hard I try, I can't shake the feeling that I'm endlessly falling in love with Johnathan Ronsberry.

CHAPTER 29

Johnathan

I DON'T WANT this moment to end. The last of the lust faded a while ago as I lay on the leather couch with Kylie in my arms. If things were different, I could lay like this forever. But life isn't that kind to a guy like me.

"Is there any more pizza left?" She looks up at me, those dark eyes glowing in the night.

"Why are you always so hungry?" I laugh.

She shrugs, flipping onto her stomach to face me. "Can't a girl be hungry without being questioned?"

"Not when she just ate half of a pie by herself," I tease, and she slaps my arm with a laugh.

I could get used to this. Once this case is over, Kylie and I will be able to do whatever we want. We could lounge at my apartment for once instead of this stuffy office. There we can really do whatever we want without any prying eyes. I can already see me pinning her again the shower wall as the lust returns.

Kylie stares at me with an easy smile. "What are you thinking about?"

"Just imaging life after this case is over." I sigh, running my fingers through her hair.

"Good, because I meant what I said before. I think you have Leo and Isabella cornered with this evidence."

The belief in her eyes is infectious, and I kiss her to steel my nerves. I have to believe in this just as much as she does, or it won't work. Her kisses hold me captive, and I wrap my arms around her. Grabbing that sweet ass stirs my urges awake completely, and I let her slip out of my grasp long enough to switch our positions. She lays there before me, and I hover over her. I know I should go over those files one more time before we call it a night, but that will have to wait for the moment. Her legs wrap around me, and the smell of her is invitation enough. I move to unzip my pants to start round two, but the ring of the company phone stops me in my tracks.

"Seriously?" I groan, climbing off Kylie. Even in the middle of the night I have no peace.

"Hello?"

"Johnathan." Leonardo's voice sends ice through my veins. "How is my favorite workaholic doing?"

"Oh, you know me." I chuckle awkwardly. "Always looking for a new way to stay ahead of the game."

"It makes me so happy to hear you say that," he says. "I'd like you take a break for a while and come meet me in my office. I want to talk to you before the celebration of life ceremony tomorrow. Isa has instructed me to have some papers for you ready to sign."

I'm terrified. Has he caught wind of the plan before it's even begun?

"Of course. I'll be right down!" I say, hanging up before he can say more.

Kylie waits for me back on the couch, and I wish that we could just pick up where we left off. But the plan must be executed perfectly. That includes convincing Leo that I'm not a threat.

I sigh and adjust my clothes. "Party's over."

"Was that Leo?" she asks, eyes wide with concern.

There's no way I'm involving her with anything else. Any closer and she would be in serious trouble. I run a hand through my hair and shrug on my jacket. "Just a business partner scheduling a meeting. Nothing I can't handle. I'll call a car to take you home."

"Okay."

I can tell she isn't fully convinced but doesn't press the issue. I do my best to seem casual as she composes herself and slings her bag over her shoulder.

"I'll see you here tomorrow." She smiles at me.

I return her smile the best I can before she walks out the door. Once this is all over, I'll focus on

Kylie. But for now, I have a meeting with the devil himself.

I ROLL up to the Guerra family house, the outside looking more ominous than it does in the daytime. A few of the windows sit with bars, and I shudder at the thought of being trapped in there with Leo. Do I really have to go inside?

My driver opens the door, and I step out into the misty night. One of Leo's men stands at the entryway holding the door open for me, and I shuffle inside. Time to get this over with.

The man leads me into the living room where Leo sits in a large, leather armchair. The pelt of a cheetah hangs on the backwall, and he rises to greet me, his meaty hands outstretched toward me.

"Johnathan! Glad you made it on such short notice."

"Anything for family." I firmly shake his hand and follow him over to where he was seated before.

He leans back with ease as I take the couch across from him. "So, how are things, my boy?"

"Busy. I feel like the weeks just keep going."

"I feel that."

It's small talk, but he's probing. I can sense him checking for anything he needs to take care of by the look in his eye. One wrong move and I'll probably end up right next to my dad in the ground. I doubt

Isabella would mind if it meant she got to keep everything.

Leo grips the neck of the crystal liquor bottle and pours us each a drink. "I'm so glad that you and Isa came to an understanding yesterday."

"Isabella is a very persuasive woman." I nod, taking the drink. "It's hard to argue with her."

"Glad that you see it that way." He clinks my glass before leaning back to his comfortable position. "I want my daughter to have everything she desires, especially with the baby on the way."

I chug the liquor like water, trying not to choke. I can't tell if he's bluffing or not. For all I know, those two psychos actually impregnated Isabella with my sperm, and I'll have a whole different set of problems after this signing.

"It did catch me by surprise." I cough a little. "I didn't take Isabella as the mothering type."

"She is a force that will surprise you." Leo chuckles. "Just don't double cross her."

"Wouldn't dream of it."

"But honestly, I think everything is happening at a perfect time. Once the ink is dry, we can have a more in-depth conversation about some loose ends your father left between us over brunch."

"Of course."

"And I'm sure Isa will want to talk to you about living arrangements with the new bundle of joy on the way."

I count down the moments until I'm allowed to

leave as he continues to remind me of the pain they intend to cause for the next twenty years of my life. Every second I'm here, I'm reminded how helpless I really am. It's almost as if he can just snuff me out with the snap of his fingers and no one would question it. I can see why my dad was drawn to his power, but I'm starting to become more convinced that he died over more than bad cholesterol. And if I don't ace this performance, I'm next. All I need to do is survive and win the game tomorrow when there are other lawyers present. It's the only way I can get on with my life and leave my father's dirt behind me once and for all.

CHAPTER 30

Kylie

I WALK INSIDE to see Jax standing at the dinner table mumbling to himself. Even in the middle of the night he's going full force. At least the late-night interrogations have ended. The laptop sits open with latest files I've sent Jax, and I watch him scribble something onto a notepad with frustration.

"How's it going over there?" I ask, startling him.

"Kylie!" he yelps. "I didn't hear you come in."

"Any progress in your capture plan?"

"I think I've got a plan that will take down Leonardo and still manage to bail out Johnathan from having to serve jail time."

I sigh with relief. "Glad to hear it. The signing is tomorrow night, so I think Leo should be in his office before then."

"That's what I'm hoping. Did you bring the final copy of the files with you?"

"Yep." I dig in my purse and begin to panic when

I don't find it. "What? No way. Did I leave it plugged into the computer?"

"Seriously, Kylie?" Jax groans.

"Don't worry. I'll just go and grab it from the office. It's not like I'll be bothering anyone."

"Okay. But hurry back. I need to get this to David before I can make a real case against him. Without those files, my hands are completely tied."

"I'm going." I give him a thumbs-up and head back out the door.

I GLARE at the jump drive sticking out of my computer with disdain. Of all the days to forget this. I yank it out of the sleeping computer and throw the jump drive in my purse. Once I get this to Jax, Leo and Isabella will be history. I take in the office with a bit of sadness. This is probably the last time that I'll ever see it this late. Tomorrow, I'll type up my resignation letter while Johnathan is busy letting his captors down easy and hopefully life will go back to normal. Maybe Johnathan will be able to show me a bit more of New York now that he'll have full control of his schedule. I wasn't joking when I said I was slacking on my tourist to-do list. I can already see his face as I pitch him the idea of taking a ferry to the statue of liberty. If I'm really lucky, I won't even need to work too hard for a good job in real estate. Being the girl of

Johnathan Ronsberry will be recommendation enough.

I notice a few of the boxes leaning over to one side and walk over to straighten them out. The last thing I want to do on the morning of my last day is clean up a pile of papers. I manage to straighten the stack when the door creaks open. Did Johnathan also forget something? No such luck.

I swallow hard as Isabella narrows her eyes at me.

"Are you seriously still here?" she barks.

"I had forgotten something," I stammer. "I thought I'd come back here—"

"In the middle of the night? You should've just gotten it tomorrow." Her gaze shifts toward the boxes behind me. "I see you and Johnathan have been busy."

"Yes, well, Johnathan has more clients than ever these days."

"Funny because I thought the client database looked unchanged from last month."

A few men file in behind her. They are different from Johnathan's clean-cut crew. These men have scars and stories that you don't want to know about. I have to stall them and get the fuck out of here.

"Anything I can help you find?"

"What I'm looking for is none of your concern," she spits. Isabella is harsh and leaves no room for small talk. She's nothing like the sweet girl that I last saw.

"I'll get out of your way," I stammer. "I'm sure you have much to do."

Her eyes are suspicious as she walks toward me. "What are you really doing here?"

"Um…I'm not sure what you mean?" I try not to show my fear of being caught. She clearly knows something.

I'm frozen in place as she stands directly in front of me. "You're not going anywhere. Sit."

She holds out a chair from the conference table, and I numbly sit down. I need to get rid of my purse before she finds the jump drive. Isabella begins to sift through the top box, tossing it aside to look through another. Judging the distance from here to the door, I can probably sprint fast enough to make it to the elevator. But then what? I'm sure she has people waiting downstairs. Is there a back door I can take to get as far away from her as possible?

"It looks like Johnathan has been a very naughty boy." Isabella shakes her head, shutting the box and tossing it aside.

"I'm sure he's no worse than you," I mumble.

Her eyes are like ice as she walks toward me and grips my chin, her pointed nails digging into my skin. "Since you have so much to say, you and I are going to get to know each other a little better." She releases me and turns toward her men searching the room. I toss my purse under the table. Hopefully it's too dark that they won't pay it any attention.

"You two, take all of these boxes to the warehouse," she commands. "And you two, help me lead our new guest downstairs. We will be taking her to a more efficient room to get acquainted in."

I run for the door in a desperate attempt to try and lead their attention away from the table. The men are on me before I can even make it halfway across the room.

"Why are you doing this?" I ask as two men grip me hard by the arms.

Isabella smiles at me. "You'll find out soon enough. But for now, I think you look a little tired. You should rest."

The shock zaps me from the side, and I scream out in pain. My body goes limp as the two men hold me up, and I try to fight the darkness as Isabella walks away toward the elevator.

"Night-night." She laughs as my eyes begin to grow heavy.

"No," I mumble.

At least the jump drive is safe. My vision blurs as I'm consumed by the darkness and across the threshold. *I'm sorry, Johnathan. I've failed. The rest is up to you. I can only hope it will be enough.*

CHAPTER 31

Johnathan

COME ON, *Kylie. Pick up.*

I pace back and forth in my apartment, only to hear the sound of Kylie's voicemail coming to life on the other end, again. Damn. This is the third time that I've called her and she's yet to respond. I wanted to go over the plan one more time before I left for the meeting. Hopefully hearing more than her voicemail will calm my nerves. I type in the number for the office and tap my foot impatiently. Desperate times, desperate measures.

"Ronsberry Law Firm," the receptionist says.

"Hi, Cindy. Can you to patch me through to Ms. Kylie? I can't seem to get ahold of her."

"Ms. Kylie hasn't come in today."

I start to break into a sweat. "What?"

"Is there something wrong, Mr. Ronsberry?" Cindy asks.

"No, I must've gotten the day wrong," I mumble. "Thank you, Cindy."

My mind races as I hang up the phone and sit on the edge of the bed. Something must have happened to her. There's no way that Kylie would be late on a day like today. I made sure to leave her name out of anything related to this meeting down to the witnesses so Leo wouldn't suspect her. Did Isabella find something? Would Leo stoop so low as to threaten me with Kylie if Isa told him to? None of this make any sense. I grip my phone tightly as I dial Jax's number. *Please pick up.*

"Yo."

"Where's Kylie?" I practically yell. "Please tell me that she's with you."

There's a rustle of papers in the background before he responds, voice strained. "Kylie went back to the office last night because she forgot...something. I figured she just pulled another all-nighter and stayed at the office."

The pause in his voice sets off alarms in my brain. "What did you do?"

"What?" Jax laughs nervously. "Nothing. What do you mean?"

I can feel the anger rising. "I know you, Jax. You're hiding something."

"I'm not. Just...ask Kylie. She'll vouch for me."

His casual tone makes me explode. "Kylie isn't answering my calls! The receptionist hasn't seen her all day, so she's not at the office either."

"What?" Jax's voice changes to panic. "Are you sure?"

Whatever Jax is hiding must have something to do with the case.

"Meet me at the office," I say through gritted teeth. "I think it's time we've properly caught up."

"Johnathan, breathe."

I'm seeing red as I pace around the room, ready to throw things after Jax finishes explaining everything. So much for Jax being a good friend.

"I can't believe this!" I yell. "Both of you have been going behind my back this whole time?"

"Well, it was originally my idea," Jax stutters.

"And it was a shitty one. I can't believe that you put Kylie in this kind of danger."

"Me?" He scoffs. "We wouldn't be here in the first place if it wasn't for you and your father's illegal antics."

"Only because you insisted for me to hire your sister." I groan loudly, fed up with it all. "My investigation left us under the radar. Isa thought she was nothing more than the help."

I shuffle past the conference table and kick something hard. It skids to the opposite side of the room, and my anger quickly turns to fear as I recognize what it is. Along with something else.

"Where are all the boxes?"

"What?" Jax asks, irritated. "Johnathan, focus."

"I am. Kylie and I had this stack of boxes here full of evidence." I pick up Kylie's clutch from the floor. "Isabella must've caught Kylie last night and took her along with everything else."

"Are you sure?" Jax asks.

My mind clicks everything together at once. "That's why Leo wanted to have that meeting last night. It was to lure me away so Isabella can go snooping around the office."

"So, what do we do now? If you knew where she was, I could call David try and assemble a team together and storm the place. But if Isabella discovered the jump drive, it's over for all of us."

I zip open the purse and smile. "Well, that's one thing she doesn't have."

I toss Jax the jump drive, and he sighs in relief.

"Wait, who's David?"

"Don't ask…" He puts a hand up as he drops himself down into a chair. I think about asking again but quickly realize it doesn't matter anyway; Kylie is the focus here.

"Okay, but we still have no idea where she's keeping Kylie." Jax leans forward and rubs his temples as if it might help him think.

"I might know where Isa's keeping her. She usually has meetings at a place down by the docks, but you have to wait for my signal before you go there, or they could kill Kylie before you ever reach her. These guys tend to not play by normal rules."

"What's your plan?" Those words seem to rattle him a bit.

"Depends. How long will it take you to put a team together?"

Jax grabs his phone and texts someone; it chimes back in about thirty seconds. "I can have a team together in less than an hour."

"Perfect. Isabella should be meeting us at Le Chatue to sign the contract in about an hour and a half. Once she's there, I'll let you know, and you should have enough time to see if that's where she's holding Kylie."

"But what about you? Won't you have to sign the deal to stall Isabella and Leo?"

I stare out at the sea of buildings before me with a heavy sigh. "If this takedown plan of yours is as foolproof as I believe it to be, then I'll stall them long enough for you to take them down too."

"My plan didn't account for you signing the deal, Johnathan."

"I know. But it might be the only way to save Kylie." I turn toward him. "So, are you in or out?"

Jax smiles at me with a fire in his eyes. "Let's go save Kylie."

CHAPTER 32

Kylie

I WAKE up to complete darkness and the distant sounds of dripping water. Where am I? My arms ache behind me, and a quick tug tells me that I've been tied up tight to a chair. The cloth around my face leaves only enough room for my nose. I guess she didn't want to kill me just yet. I can still hear Isabella's eerie laughter as she took everything from the office, and I shudder at the thought of being tased again. Panic begins to set in. I threw my purse hoping that Johnathan would find it in the morning, but if he's going to the signing, he'll never see it. And if Isabella took all the evidence, that makes Johnathan's freedom plan useless. And without the jump drive, Jax can't put Leo away after the meeting. This is all my fault. I need to get out of here and fix this! But how?

I feebly struggle against the ropes tying my limbs,

the effort from only breathing out of my nose making me lightheaded.

"Oh look, she's awake."

The fabric is ripped off my face, and I blink back the harsh light. Isabella towers over me, smug as ever. I notice a few of her men standing behind her. What did they think I could possibly do to her in this state? The rest of the room comes into view as my vision clears. The dripping water comes from the pipes lining the ceiling and creates a puddle in the corner. Judging by the gray-colored walls and the smell of seawater, we're in some kind of fishing shed. For all I know, we could be in a completely different state. Either way, I'm nowhere near the office or Johnathan, and I'm tied up and phoneless. I'm so screwed.

"Have a nice nap?" Isabella smiles wickedly.

"Hardly."

"I'm impressed, by the way," she says, circling me. "I never would've pegged Johnathan to hire someone as plain as you to help him take us down."

"I have no idea what you're talking about."

"Oh? Do you?"

She takes her phone out of her pocket and flips the screen my way, the security footage of the office staring back at me. My cheeks are hot as I watch Johnathan press me up against the wall, the moment between us on display for me to see. How many people has she shown this to? Isabella drops her

171

phone with a look of satisfaction. This woman is pure evil, and she knows it.

"What do you want?" I ask, desperate to find a solution.

"Nothing you can offer. Although I guess I should be thanking you. With you as my hostage, I can probably negotiate an even better deal."

"Johnathan wouldn't give up his company just to save me."

"Are you sure?" She looks down at her phone and swipes across the screen before flipping it my way. "That doesn't look like a quick fling to me. What's your take on it?"

My heart hammers in my chest as I stare at a still of Johnathan and me laying on the couch, his smile genuine and loving. How did I not notice that before?

"I think that you won't get away with this." I look at her. "You can't just use people to get what you want."

"But I already have." She laughs. "Do you honestly think that all of this was my father's idea?"

"What?"

"My father is powerful, yes. But business deals are not his strength. Neither is making friends. I scouted out Johnathan at a party long before Frank and my father ever met on the putting green. Once I did a little research, it wasn't that hard to set the stage."

"So, you did all of this for what? Money? Power?" I balk. "You killed Frank Ronsberry as if he was nothing."

Her face twists in annoyance. "I didn't kill Frank. He killed himself eating those disgusting sandwiches he loved. Saved me and my father the trouble of doing it ourselves, so hooray for small miracles."

My head is spinning. I wish I had a way to record all of this and get it to Jax, but I'm helpless with these ropes tied around me. I'm nothing more than a captive audience for the Isabella show.

"I guess I should also thank you for organizing those files so nicely for us. The way that things were moving before, I was starting to think those files Frank hid were just a myth. It's a shame I have to kill you. I could've used you to clean up my father's office." Isabella's nails dig into my skin as she grips my face. "What do you say? Want to work for the bad guys for a little while?"

I open my mouth as wide as I can and bite her hand, a surge of pride flowing through me as she yelps back in pain.

"You stupid bitch!" Isabella screams as she slaps me across the face. One of her men moves in closer with a taser, but she holds up her good hand to stop them. "Leave her. We have places to be. Besides, with the storm coming in, she'll freeze soon enough."

With all the adrenaline pumping through me, I didn't even notice I'm not wearing anything but my work attire. Isabella glares at me as she rips off a piece of my shirt and ties it around her hand. "Put the tape on her mouth and let's get out of here. I don't want to keep Johnathan waiting."

No. She can't leave. I try to think of something to keep her here, but my mind draws a blank. What can stop a woman so evil?

"Is this how you plan to raise your child?" I yell as the guys close in on me. "This isn't a good environment to raise anyone in. Don't you want them to have a good life?"

Isabella stops, and I smile. I've got her. I guess she isn't heartless after all. But as she slowly turns to face me, my confidence plummets, and I'm terrified of the look on her face. The evilest look lingers in her eyes as she rubs her flat stomach.

"Do I look like the kind of person who would do anything to mess up this gorgeous body? You're just as naïve as Johnathan. No wonder he chose someone like you."

The tape is smeared on my mouth, and Isabella ushers her goons away. I try to scream, but the tape traps it inside. The fear bubbles up fast as Isabella closes the door and the lock clicks shut. I can't let her get away with this. I teeter back and forth, trying to break free of these bonds. All I need is my hands and I'll be able to get free. Then I can get to Johnathan and...

My balance leans to one side, and I fall hard to the ground. With no hands to brace my fall, my head slams hard into the concrete, my vision and blurs and disorients. No. I can't black out now. I need to help Johnathan before it's too late. No matter how hard I try, I can't fight it, and the darkness swallows me once more.

CHAPTER 33

Johnathan

THE WIND WHIPS through my jacket as I wait outside for Isabella. Of course she would pick the day of the most snow we've seen in months to set up this meeting. Did she pay off the weather too? I look down at my phone and text Jax an update, telling him to stand by. There's no guarantee that Isa would be cocky enough to leave Kylie unguarded, but as long as she was here with me, I could at least track her movements.

The car rolls up, and I shove my phone into my pocket, moving from my comfortable stance on the wall. Looks like it's showtime.

Isabella emerges dressed in all black, a white muff covering both her hands. A dark empress ready to claim her kingdom. I watch as she walks past me without a single greeting, those lips pursed in a twisted scowl. For someone who's about to get everything she wants, she doesn't look too happy about it. I can't really remember a time that Isa was happy about anything, but today seems like that kind of occasion.

I follow silently behind her, the dining hall alive with live music and the smell of food. This celebration of life party seemed like it had heavy accents on the celebration part.

"Johnathan!" Leonardo yells, face flushed as he walks toward me through the crowd. "Glad you could make it."

He wraps a heavy arm around my shoulders, and I force a smile. "Wouldn't miss it for the world, sir."

"Come. Let's get you a drink to celebrate!"

He leads me toward the bar, the usual set up of chairs and tables pushed aside for his guests to mingle. Are all these people in on the plan, or are they just innocent bystanders covering up his latest scheme? I glance back at Isabella, who's whispering to one of her men. He nods at her before leaving back out the door, and I try not to panic. There has to be a way to text Jax before we run out of time.

"All right, what can I get you?" Leo grunts, shaking me a little. "Anything you want is on me tonight."

"I'll take a rum and Coke." I smile, whipping out my phone. "How about take a photo to celebrate this occasion? I need some new ones for my office, and I don't want to look too drunk to my clients."

"Absolutely," Leo cheers, hugging me closer. His voice dips low as I set up the camera. "If you do anything to fuck this up, I'll end you where you stand. You know that, right?"

"Wouldn't dream of it," I say, holding up the camera in front of us. "Say, 'money.'"

"Money!" Leo cheeses for the camera and finally lets me go, grabbing our drinks.

I quickly send Jax a thumbs-up text and shoot the photo to Leo. "There, now you have a copy for your office."

"Lovely." He hands me my drink, eyes cautious. "Who better to surround yourself with than family on a day like today? Am I right?"

I hold up my drink. "To family."

He clinks my glass, and I nearly chug the whole drink in one gulp. Hopefully the rum will calm my nerves long enough to get through this thing. I know I told Jax that signing everything away is no big deal, but the thought of even holding a pen right now seems impossible. Even if it is to save Kylie.

"Johnathan," Isabella calls for me. "A word?"

I down the rest of my drink and slam the glass on the bar. "Coming."

My heart is beating overtime, fear slowly encroaching the closer I get to her. The look in her eyes tells me that whatever she wants to talk about, it's nothing good. I follow her through the throng of people toward the bathrooms, the shadowed hall anything but comforting.

"What do you want, Isa?" I spit.

"I want more than fifty percent."

"You're fucking with me." I laugh, nearly mad. "How much more could you want?"

"I want seventy percent and full control of future partnerships. Clearly Ronsberry Law Firm has an issue with who they do business with."

"Clearly."

She shakes her head, a small smile on her lips. "You can jab me all you want. But a company like Ronsberry has no need for a leader who doesn't know how to keep business and pleasure separate."

One of her hands emerges from the muff with her phone, the surveillance footage of the office on the screen. I blanch as the video plays out my desires.

"Where did you get this?" I ask, voice strained.

Isabella's hand falls, and her smile broadens. "Does it matter? I have everything I need to make sure that you don't slip up and ruin my plans."

"Your plans?"

"I'm having the contract drafted for seventy percent as we speak. Sign it, or this video goes online, and you'll become the scumbag who cheated on his pregnant wife with his assistant. I'm sure the courts won't have a problem handing over everything after that."

Isabella turns away with pride, a bit of red cloth peeking out of her muff as she hides her hand. I catch a metallic scent as she walks away, and I grip onto the wall to steady myself. Blood. Is she really parading around with it in her muff? Did she already kill Kylie? I want to yank out my phone and call Jax, but that will ruin the whole operation. All I can do is wait patiently and trust him. I walk back out into the dining room and politely squeeze my way back to the bar. I'm going to need another drink if I'm going to survive this.

"There he is!"

Leo stands across the room with Isabella, waving me over with the widest of smiles. "Come here, son. We have much to discuss."

I gulp down my fears and wave back with a nod. Time to sell away my soul.

CHAPTER 34

Kylie

IT'S SO COLD. I blink through the pain as I regain consciousness, the side of my head still leaning on the cold cement. I wiggle my fingers to get the blood circulating, but they feel completely numb. Am I really going to die here? It doesn't seem like there's anyone else here, and I use whatever strength I have left to get on my knees. Maybe I can manage to smash the chair apart with my weight. They do it all the time in movies. The chances of me impaling myself are pretty high, but if Scarlett Johansson can do it, then so can I. Johnathan is probably at his meeting right now. Depending on where I am, maybe I can get there in time. Then I—

The lock of the door clicks open, disrupting my thoughts. I turn my head just enough to see one of Isa's goons walking toward me as the door slams closed. I was so sure that Isabella was cocky enough to just let me freeze to death that I never considered she would send someone to finish the job. I'm numb with fear as he gets closer, the black bag rustling in his hand. There's no way that I can die here. Everything that I've worked for and sacrificed isn't about to be snuffed out by some tattooed guy in a warehouse. Especially not at the orders of that bitch. There's no way I can run or even fight back this way, and my mind is too fuzzy to come up with a plan. I'm too afraid to even scream as he reveals his gun, the tears falling freely down my face. This really is the end. His eyes are cold with no emotion as he moves closer.

"It's nothing personal, kid."

"Put your hands up!"

The sound of heavy boots and radio chatter fills the air as two cops storm the room, their guns pointed at my almost killer.

"Drop it!"

The man drops the gun instantly as the cop presses one against his temple.

This almost feels like a dream. My vision is too blurred by tears to make out the figure running toward me until he's right in front of me. His face is contorted in a mix of pain and relief.

"Kylie, I'm so sorry," Jax sobs, hugging me tight. "I should've never gotten you involved in any of this."

I can't help but lean into him and cry, the fear of death still lingering. He pulls away and gently pulls the tape from my mouth. I feel someone else working through the ropes as I flex my jaw a little.

"Thanks," I croak. "How did you find me?"

"Johnathan noticed you were missing and called me. After I told him everything, he managed to piece the rest together and told us about this place. We had to make sure Isabella was gone before we made our move."

I look past Jax. "Where's Johnathan now?"

"He's probably signing away his life right now," Jax says, face grim. "He thought it was the best way to distract Isabella and Leo."

"What?" I wince at my sore limbs as they're released from the ropes, and I collapse fully onto the floor.

"Don't worry." Jax sighs. "David has sent a team to arrest Leo. You were smart to throw your purse, by the way."

I'm relieved to know that I was able to help, but it's not enough to quell my worries about Johnathan. Once he signs those papers, he's just as much as a criminal as his father.

"We have to stop Johnathan," I croak, trying to find the strength to stand.

"You are going with the medical team to get checked out," he orders. "I'm going over there as backup, so you don't need to worry."

"A medical team can check me on the way there," I snap. "I'm not letting you leave without me."

"I don't think you're in any position to negotiate right now."

"You owe me," I say, flexing my fingers a little.

"You wouldn't even have gotten this far if it wasn't for me. You said that."

Jax groans and shakes his head in frustration. "Kylie—"

"I love him, Jax," I blurt out. "If he's going to go down for saving me, the least you can let me do is say goodbye."

He studies me, face twisted. There's no guarantee that Jax can offer immunity to Johnathan after he signs those papers, and he knows it. And we're running out of time.

"Fine!" he finally yells, looking past me. "Carry her to the van and check her vitals. We're going against the clock here, so let's move."

I wince as they lift me up and do my best to stay still. Every part of me hurts, and I would love nothing more than to lay back and let a bunch of nurses cater to my aching limbs and sandpaper throat. But there are more important things on the line. I wouldn't put it past Isabella to order Johnathan's car to crash after he leaves the signing. The thought of losing Johnathan forever scares me more than anything else. Seeing him again alive is what fuels me to move past the pain. The engine revs to life, and I'm laid on the floor of the van. The medical team hovers over me as the van rolls forward. *Hold on a little longer, Johnathan. I'm coming.* I just only hope we're not too late.

CHAPTER 35

Johnathan

THIS IS IT. No turning back now.

I follow Leo and Isabella into a windowless room and the din of the party fades as one of their men closes the door. A table set up in the middle of the floor, and I spot my lawyer and chosen witness stand uncomfortably in the corner. The statement they're trying to make is clear. I have no power here.

"Sorry for the formalities, son," Leo says. "It's a habit of mine to not mix emotions with business. You understand, don't you?"

"Of course," I say, mouth dryer than ever.

I take my seat across from Isa and her father, the two of them looking smug as they sign the contract laid out in front of them. Leo hands the pen to his daughter and Isa takes it with her nondominant hand.

"Something wrong with your hand?" I say, eyeing the white muff.

"I'm embarrassed to say I sprained my wrist doing yoga." She sighs and takes her time signing her name. Whatever she's hiding might buy me a little more time, but by the look of the guards spread out around the room, I shouldn't press the issue.

Leo spins the document to face me and holds out a pen. "Your turn, my boy."

I take the pen, mind racing to come up with anything to stall. "I think I should take the time to read through this since it was recently revised."

"Now, Johnathan," Leo starts.

"Oh, let him read it, Daddy," Isabella sneers. "No harm in double checking that they spelled my name right."

The more that I read, the sicker I become. Once I sign this paper, my company will be merged with their underground cooperation. Everything down to the dollar will be entangled in Leo's money laundering and Isabella's schemes. I want to usher my lawyer over and demand he renegotiate, but the chances of him getting killed to prove a point are high.

My hand won't stop trembling as I pick up the pen, and I hear Isa chuckle under her breath. She's enjoying my misery of being backed into this corner. I'm all out of moves, and she's about to win it all.

"What are you waiting for, Johnathan?" Leo grumbles impatiently.

I take a deep breath and shrug back my shoulders. If it's to save Kylie, it's worth it. My pen hovers over the paper as a commotion breaks out in the dining hall.

"What is going on?" Leo gestures for two of his men to scope it out, but the police bust down the door before they have the chance. I duck under the desk as someone fires the first shot, and soon, its total chaos. Bullets rain down on the desk as I do my best to stay out of the fray. I hear Leonardo yell in the distance, and the bullets slowly stop.

"Get his hands!" an officer yells. "You are under arrest."

I watch in disbelief as the cops pin a large guy like Leonardo Guerra to the ground, cuffing his hands behind his back. Isabella tries to run but has been backed into a corner, her mascara running as they snap the handcuffs in place.

"Johnathan?"

The sound of Kylie's voice makes my heart soar, and I crawl out of my hiding spot to see her standing in the doorway. Kylie runs into my arms, and I hold her close.

"You're alive," I breathe, staring at those dark eyes full of tears.

"So are you." She laughs with relief as the tears fall.

I look past her at Jax entering the room, and he holds up a hand in triumph. "We did it."

"Barely." I shake my head and give him a high five.

"Did you sign the contract?" Kylie asks, still clinging to me.

"No. You guys happen to have impeccable timing."

"That still doesn't mean that you're in the clear, but it's better than jail time." Jax pats me on the shoulder. "I'll ask them to give you two a moment before they take you in for questioning."

"Thanks, Jax." I smile a little.

He nods before walking away, and I look down at Kylie all bandaged up, and it makes me feel nauseous. If it wasn't for me, none of this would have happened and she would be safe doing some basic job downtown. I can't go through this again; who knows? Next time, it could end far worse. As much as I want to just whisk her away, I don't want to involve her in my messes anymore. And knowing Leo and Isabella, this mess clearly isn't over. After this fiasco, it's obvious she has a target on her back that won't be going away as long as she's attached to me. And if I know Leo or Isa, they will have someone in the wings waiting to swoop in and take their temporary reign, while they call the shots.

"I'm so happy that you're okay," I say, letting go of her. "But I think we should talk."

Her face falls, and she takes a step back. "About what?"

"About us. I think that after what's just happened, we should go our separate ways."

"What?" She balks. "I just risked my life for you and you're just calling it quits?"

"You lied to me," I whisper fiercely. This was also weighing heavily on my mind. "The entire time we were working together, you were feeding your brother all the information."

"It was to help you."

"It was a lie. And I'm through with being lied to. I'm sorry, Kylie."

I walk away from her before I lose my resolve, her eyes staring at me as I walk toward Jax.. Even though it breaks my heart to end it like this with Kylie, it's better this way. She was supposed to just be a getaway fling anyway. I have to let her go; it's what's best for her. But as I'm lead farther and farther away from her, I know that's anything but the truth.

CHAPTER 36

Kylie

IT'S OVER? It can't be.

I replay Johnathan's words in my mind ad nauseum as Jax drives us home after a long day of questioning. Maybe there's a hidden message behind them that I missed. There's no way that he can just drop me like that after all we've been through. But, as I return my badge and the weeks go on, I don't hear a word from him. Unless it's the information I'm prying out of Jax about the ongoing investigation, I have no idea what Johnathan's up to. Jax was able to strike up a deal where Johnathan offered immunity for turning all of his information over to the attorney general's office. Which means the police will continue to dig through the company from top to bottom. It's intrusive, but it prevents Johnathan from being wrapped up in any more schemes. Plus, it keeps him safe from any vengeful associates the Guerra Family might have lingering in the shadows.

Two weeks pass, and I find myself sleeping and eating more. I chalk it up to a broken heart and my period coming on and continue to mope around the house. No job, no Johnathan, and the lack of nutrition in my diet has me running to the bathroom more than I want to. So much for taking over New York.

"WHAT?" This can't be happening right now as I stare down at the little stick in my hand. My whole body goes numb, my heart racing. This is not the way I imagined this happening at all. But frankly none of this is. I never thought when I moved to New York, I'd become part of a criminal investigation, fall in love, be kidnapped, and dumped all within a few short months. Now this.

The more I replay the evens in my head, the more my sadness transforms into rage. After everything I've done to help him, this is how he repays me? I manage to find his address in Jax's files and make my move. Enough of the silence. It's my turn to talk now.

I STAND in front of his apartment building, frozen from fear and the cold. What if he rejects me on the doorstep? The anger inside has dulled to a low roar, and I force myself to walk into the lobby. I've already made it this far. There's no sense getting cold feet at the last second. I punch the button to the eighth floor and watch the elevator doors close with a combination of excitement and fear. It hasn't been that long since I've seen him, but it doesn't make my insides stir any less. I make my way down the hall and muster up the last of my courage as I bang on his door.

"Coming."

His voice makes my heart do a back flip. I can hear him shuffling on the other side, and I'm practically vibrating with anticipation by the time the door swings open. Johnathan stares at me in disbelief, his usual business attire replaced with sweatpants and a gray t-shirt.

"Kylie? What are you doing here?" Truthfully, he doesn't look well, which makes me a little happy inside.

"I've come to talk to you," I say, the anger slowly rising. "May I come in?"

He steps back and lets me inside, the faint sound of fake warfare blaring in the distance. I take in the modest décor and minimal furniture. For a man of many riches, he lives a normal-looking life.

"You look well," he says, looking sheepish.

"No thanks to you," I spit.

"Kylie, I'm sorry for the way everything happened." He's trying to be stern, but he's lying to me; I can see it in his eyes.

"No." I stop him. "You're not sorry at all. It's been two weeks, and I've heard nothing from you."

"Are you serious?" He balks. "I've literally been in meetings and interrogations since the last time I saw you. I can't even go to the office; the press is all over the place."

I glance at him again, trying to make sense of what he's saying. I feel like I'm getting mixed messages. He's trying to keep his distance, but it looks like he's trying almost too hard.

"You still could've called."

"I was trying to leave you out of all of this."

"Too late for that, don't you think?"

"Kylie," he pleads. "I'm just trying to make sure that you're safe. I can't drag you in to any more of this mess."

"I let you in!" I yell. "I told myself that after my ex-husband I was done with love. But you changed that. And I thought that after everything we've been through, I thought things would be different."

"They are!" he yells back. "Leo and Isa are locked away, I'm a prisoner in my own apartment, and the feds are combing through every file of the firm."

"You know that's not what I mean!"

Rage flares up inside me, and I grab a book off a nearby shelf and hurl it at him.

"Kylie, stop!" he yells as I find more things to throw.

Who cares if I break something? He's got money coming out of his ears. And here I am penniless.

He walks through my barrage and grips my wrists, staring me in the eye. "What do you want from me?"

I try my best to wiggle myself free. But he just moves closer and backs me up against the bookshelf. He presses my arms to my sides, and I can see it in his eyes: he loves me too. As his look changes from confusion to desire, he leans in and whispers in my ear, "What do you want from me, Kylie?"

I am weak in the knees. This can't be all in my head; I know he can feel the intensity between us. I want him. Why doesn't he want me too? I sob, unable to keep my emotions in check anymore. "I want you to be a good father."

Johnathan bolts back, and the color drains from his face as he lets go. "What?"

I take in a shaky breath and find the courage to say it out loud.

"I'm pregnant."

CHAPTER 37

Johnathan

My body is numb and my eyes are glued to Kylie's tearstained face. The phrase echoes in my head over and over, but I can't find any words to respond.

Pregnant.

My brain tries to reboot as my emotions rock from excited to terrified all at once. With the investigation still going on, this isn't the best time to bring something so pure and innocent into the world. Especially after I've done my best to stay away from Kylie in the first place. With all the connections the Guerra Family has, I'm sure they want someone to pin the blame of their recent arrest on. And I'm the perfect target. Jax and David have tried to assure me it won't happen with all of the evidence we've given them. But I still feel uneasy nonetheless.

Clearly I'm not going to be winning any father of the year awards. I think back to how I've handled myself. I swallow hard, trying to bring life back to my body.

Kylie leans against the bookshelf, visibly exhausted. My arms numbly reach for a nearby chair and drag it closer.

"Here. Sit."

"You look like you need it more than me." She smirks a little.

I breathe out a shaky laugh and shake my head. She's not wrong. Me? A father? I drag over another chair for myself and nearly collapse onto the cushion. Kylie eyes me before taking the chair across from me.

"How long have you known?"

"Since this morning, actually," she says, holding her hands in her lap. "I'm still super pissed at you for ditching out on me like you did...but I wanted you to be the first to know."

She's killing me. All I've wanted to do since meeting Kylie is hold her in my arms and never let her go. I'm sure I look like crap after wasting the days here feeling sorry for myself. Being in front of someone in anything other than a suit feels uncomfortable. Except for when I'm around Kylie, of course. If anything, I want as minimal clothing between us as possible. And even through the numbness all the feelings I have for her come flooding back, making my body respond in ways that are not appropriate right now.

"Well, thank you," I stammer, unsure what else to say. My head is spinning with guilt, being mad at myself for what I've done the last few weeks, and the scent of Kylie that I've missed so much I'm having a hard time concentrating.

Her face falls a little. "You're welcome."

"So, what do you want to do? I know your move to New York didn't have baby on the list."

"It didn't have a lot of things on this list," she muses. "I think it's safe to say my plans have all gone to shit and I need a new one."

"Any ideas?"

"Depends."

"On?" She blinks at me, and my heart speeds up. Right. I clear my throat. "Ah, yes. Well."

"You don't have to be a part of this if you don't want to," she says quickly. "I know a baby wasn't on your list either."

That had me reeling a bit. To think she was already expecting me to wipe my hands clean of all this...

"Yeah, well, my list was shit to begin with." I stand and cross over to her, taking her by the hand and pulling her up to me. "Until I found you. And the only reason I pushed you away is because I thought it would be the only way to keep you safe and happy. But these last few weeks have been miserable for me."

"Really?" She tries to hide a smile, but the thought of my misery peps her up a little.

"Yes, really." Seeing her now makes me realize even more what an ass I've been. "I want you by my side. I want you and our baby to know that I'm not going anywhere."

I hope she realizes how serious I am. I would never leave her to take on the kind of responsibility alone.

Her eyes well up, and she asks softly, "What made you change your mind? The baby?"

"No. Well, yes, but no." I know what she is thinking. "I knew I made a mistake right away, but I was hoping it would get easier." I smile and wrap my arms around her waist, pulling her closer. "But it didn't. It just got harder and harder, and by that time, I was sure you'd moved on and I didn't want to upset your life by coming back into it."

"You know I don't like people make decisions for me, especially when they say it's for my own good." She wraps her arms around my neck, drawing me closer.

"Oh, I know." I kiss her lightly on the cheek.

"And you know you screwed up, right?"

I kiss her on the neck. "Oh, I do. Big time."

"Well, I think maybe it should be my job to think for the both of us because you look a mess." She laughs as she leans her head back while I continue to kiss down her throat.

"I totally agree." I kiss her lips lightly as I feel her relax into my body.

"Johnathan." She pulls back.

"Yes?" I want to devour her right here and now.

"You need a shower." We both laugh out loud.

As I sweep her up into my arms, I can't believe how lucky I am she is so damn stubborn. I whisper in her ear, "I couldn't agree more. Especially with you joining me."

I carry her down the hallway to my bathroom suite, kick the clothes out of the way, and turn the shower on. "Oh my…" She looks around in surprise at the piles of laundry on the floor.

"Look at me." I pull her face to meet mine. "Kylie, I screwed up. I've missed you. I never want to be without you again." Tears fill her eyes. "Please forgive me."

"Promise me you won't doubt our love again."

"Never. In a million years, never again."

I pull her close and kiss her deeply. The warmth of her pussy presses against my hardened cock, and I pull her shirt over her head. She's even more beautiful than I remember. She pulls down my sweatpants quickly, and it's not too long before we step into the shower, letting the warm water fall over our bodies. I turn her around and press her lightly up against the glass while a rub her breasts and press my cock against her ass.

"Mmmm…" She moans in a whisper as I kiss her neck again. My god, I've missed her. Her moans make me rock hard, so I need to pull back before it's over too quickly. I turn her back around and feel the curves of her body until my hand moves between her legs. We are both wet from the water, but I can feel her desire as I slide my finger inside her.

"Does that feel good?" I whisper.

"Yes…" she says quietly and buries her head in my chest.

I move my finger deeper, and she starts to squirm. Her hips begin to rock against my hand while I move another finger inside and pick up the pace slightly. "Oh my god, Johnathan! I can't…"

"You can't what?" I love that I can make her squirm like this.

"I need you…"

"You need me what?" I smile, very pleased with myself.

Just then, she grabs my aching member with one hand and pulls me to her, which startles me as my emotions move quickly from amusement to desperate desire. She lines my cock up with her pussy and rubs the tip against her opening. I can feel the silky wetness coating us both. Just then, she pulls my ass toward her enough to slide my cock deep inside.

"Fuck!" I don't mean to yell, but I can't help it.

"Does that feel good?" she whispers.

I want to laugh at how she flipped control around just like that, but all I can do is think of how badly I want her. "I can't…"

"Do it! Cum with me!" she yells, and just then we both find ourselves pulsating in ecstasy.

THIS WAS a night I will never forget, I think to myself as I stare at Kylie sleeping peacefully in my bed again. The most beautiful woman I've ever seen. The mother of my unborn child. My love, my heart. The more it sinks in, the lighter I feel. I smile and kiss her lightly on the forehead. Even with so much uncertainty before us, I know one thing is for sure: I'm never letting Kylie go ever again. Let the world have whatever they want. I don't care. I'm finally free. And Kylie is forever mine.

Before You Go...

If you enjoyed my book please leave a short review. These reviews help me as an author to be found by other amazing readers like you.

Thank you so much! :)

About J. J. Love

JJ Love is a steamy romance author who loves to write about Billionaire & Mafia Romantic Suspense.

She loves her coffee, hanging out at the beach, and traveling.

Keep up with all things Instant Billionaire here: https://www.facebook.com/groups/jj.love.author

Download Mystery Woman - 12 Months Later (bonus scene from Instant Billionaire): https://dl.bookfunnel.com/925my28kre

About Simone Fox

Simone Fox is a steamy romance author who loves to write about sexy bad boys.

When she's not working on her next book, she's traveling or hanging out with family.

Keep up with all things Lured here ➜ https://www.facebook.com/groups/simone.fox

www.ingramcontent.com/pod-product-compliance
Lightning Source LLC
Chambersburg PA
CBHW020412210626
46816CB00006BB/2243